CW00524813

Time

Fly

Paul E Casino

DEDICATION

This book is dedicated to Henry George Parker-Lyon,
Simon, and Camilla's son, to wish him all the very best on
his journey through what will surely be a fabulous life.

CONTENTS

Preface
1 The day job
2 Green Rivers
3 Professor Friedrich von Shultz
4 Joshua Phipps
5 Construction
6 Phipps meets Palmer
7 Bad news travels fast
8 The flying machine
9 Yes or no
10 Lanthaneodinium
11 The decision
12 The journey
13 Prison Riot
14 After the storm
15 Smuggler
16 Smallz
17 Ice cream
18 Hanks Printer Repair
19 A new day
20 Back to school
21 Lessons from the past
22 Lifers
23 Second thoughts
24 Needles
25 A new discovery
26 The tunnel
27 Carpet jungle
28 Operation Shagpile
29 An unexpected guest
30 An outdoor Flight

CONTENTS

31 Herb
32 Elvis
33 The past is over
34 The Gauntlet
35 Serial help
36 Up to her neck
37 The operation
38 Elspeth's journey
39 Hideout spy
40 The Spider
41 The Presidential Suite
42 The Gardener
43 The Preacher
44 Ashes
45 Homecoming
46 First contact
47 CCTV
48 The meet
49 The call
50 Boomerang
51 Flashdrive
52 Retirement

ACKNOWLEDGMENTS

With special thanks to my parents Roy and Liz who put up with me whilst writing this book. To my Sister Nicki for all the long walks whilst writing. To Jasmin De Vivo, my Goddaughter for the initial proofread. To Lola and Cyrus for being fabulous. To my dear friend Benny for all the support and encouragement. And finally, to my dear friend Simon Parker for all his help and support.

PREFACE

In the year 2153, time travel first became possible. Travellers could go back in time but only return to the present date, so were unable to predict or experience the future. There was great enthusiasm amongst politicians and scientists, as it was thought that past mistakes and atrocities could be rectified by returning to their origin and changing things for the better.

But there was a problem. Each time they attempted to alter the course of events; they changed the future in ways they could not have predicted. If a traveller interacted with someone from the past, even in the slightest way, history would adjust, sometimes with dramatic consequences in the present.

The perils of time travel were discussed at great length and an example was often used of Mrs Miggins from flat B, 22 Buckingham Place, Brighton, who bumped into a traveller whilst walking to the train station. The interaction only lasted for a split second but, the delay caused her to be run over by, rather than narrowly avoid, the number 27 bus, bound for Rottingdean. As a result, the bus driver committed suicide, 53 years before he was supposed to die and more importantly, without fathering two children, one of whom would later go on to win The Nobel Prize for creating a vaccine that saved millions. The ramifications for Mrs Miggins, by comparison, were less severe to mankind but, even the slightest changes made to the past affected the future dramatically, and sometimes catastrophically.

Very quickly, travellers became more focused on rectifying

past actions than doing things to try and secure a better future. The concern, a very real one, was that one of these changes could affect the future so dramatically that there would be no future at all. In early 2154, just eight months after the program was launched, it was abandoned, and time travel was outlawed globally.

A few outliers, who had the money and the resources, continued nevertheless but were quickly exposed. Their changes to the future were obvious and were tracked back to each source, perpetrators punished, and equipment confiscated and destroyed.

Despite this, there was widespread belief that governments were still using the technology to make minor tweaks to events a few days or even hours and minutes prior to the present. However, these changes were so subtle that it was difficult, even impossible, to detect or prove. In short, the further back you travelled, the more dramatically the chances were of affecting the present.

The world in 2154 was a very different place to a few hundred years before. Global warming had taken its toll, resulting in weather extremes and mass food shortages caused by over population. Resources of every type were scarce, and scientists had turned their attention to solving these problems for the good of mankind.

Efforts were focused on taking samples of the resources available and, using cutting-edge technology, making them bigger. Scientists soon discovered though that through trial and error this was impossible. However, by reverse engineering the same technology, they had no problem making things smaller for short periods and so an idea was hatched which, it was thought at the time, could solve the world's problems.

A programme began to shrink people, which later became known as "The Big Shrink". It started with all those serving time in prison and in the end, governments were paying people to become shrunk.

A 'shrink' would last for about six hours and those serving time were continually kept just the right amount shrunk until they had served out their sentence.

Those choosing to be shrunk were housed in miniature luxurious hotel, leisure and entertainment facilities and the longer you stayed that size, the cheaper it was, as the benefits far outweighed the costs. Many people chose to be shrunk as a way of life and spent months, and even years, in a state of 'shrunkenness'.

The benefits were obvious; a fully functional prison, no larger than a standard block of butter, could house thousands of inmates with all the associated costs shrunk too. At last, in every corner of the globe, the population was becoming smaller!

Green River 5, a larger than normal prison facility, sat in a hermetically sealed and temperature-controlled glass dome on its own table in the middle of warden, Joshua Phipps' office on the 13th floor of a nondescript, heavily guarded, building somewhere in New York. Phipps sat at his desk every day watching large monitors which filmed the activities of all the inmates of Green River 5 and many other prisons, all set up in the same way about his office. Phipps was not alone, other wardens had similar set ups in their offices on the same floor. The entire American penitentiary system, made up of almost 2,000 prisons, and over two and a half million inmates, guards and ancillary staff were managed from the 13th floor, all the wardens watching all the inmates, all of the time.

One such inmate was Captain Jack Palmer, a former army pilot, who had retired from The Marines to start a successful career in business, earning him millions. It had gained him great notoriety until he was caught carrying out illegal time travel activities after the ban. No release date was ever published for him or fellow inmates who had committed such crimes, as those in the justice system considered this band of men, and women, had illegally cheated time in the first place.

Jack and his crew, along with other time travel offenders were kept separate from the other inmates on the East wing of Green River 5 and they spent their time telling stories of their adventures in time travel. Warden Phipps always paid special attention to the east wing.

Nobody knew why Jack Palmer risked everything to travel back to the past and nobody asked. He carried himself in a way that only a man who has had a life and seen a lot would carry himself. He wasn't intimidating but rather assured and in control, was softly spoken and slow to anger, but he could handle himself, a true leader, a man who would get the very best from you and someone you would not wish to disappoint. Jack ran things on the east wing.

But why did this man risk everything to travel back in time, a man who had a great life and a bright future? Only time would tell.

1
THE DAY JOB

Warden Phipps finished his day as he always did at precisely 5:47pm, packing his briefcase, grabbing his coffee flask, and heading home via the subway. Leaving the 13th floor was a military operation. The exit had a shrink machine, rather like a metal detector you would commonly see at airport security. Each of the wardens' departures were staggered at 10-minute intervals and Phipps allotted time was 5:57pm. Before he could leave, he would hand over to another warden, generally Harry Williams, who would enter his office at 5:50pm precisely. They would exchange pleasantries, as they always did, a word about the preceding shift before Phipps made for the door.

"Hey Josh" said Harry, *"8 bells?"*

"8 bells Harry!", said Phipps.

8 bells referred to the eight glass domes in the office housing The Green River prisons one to eight. It was also a mariner's term used in bygone times, whereby 8 bells were rung signifying everything was as it should be on a sailing vessel, 8 bells and all's well. Phipps and Williams shared an interest in the sea, and they certainly ran a tight ship.

There was one other warden responsible for The Green River setup, Warden Walter P Courage, a surly man, who neither Phipps nor Williams cared for much. Together, these three oversaw the daily 24-hour surveillance of the facilities. Shifts moved around and temporary wardens came in to cover holidays, but Phipps pretty much always had the 10:00am till 6:00pm slot.

Wardens arriving for the shift change went through a vigorous security procedure before entering the 13th floor via a lift which would only carry passengers up and would not descend unless completely empty, another of the many security features. If a shrunk prisoner were to escape from one of the domes, an impossible feat in the first place, then manage to scale down the sheer drop from tabletop to floor, they would have to contend, from their miniature perspective, with miles of manmade jungle, as the entire 13th floor was covered in thick, shagpile carpet. The designers had thought of everything, the whole building was a fortress, the 13th another and each glass dome within it one more still. Escape impossible.

"Same time tomorrow Josh," said Harry,

Phipps nodded and made his way out. At exactly 5:57pm Phipps pressed the intercom at the shrink machine portal, it crackled into life.

"Go ahead," said the faceless voice.

"Warden Joshua Phipps, shift number 15,894 complete, permission to leave the facility?"

"Please hold," said the box.

The shrink machine was powered down, the whirring slowly decreased to silence, and a green light illuminated from the ceiling above.

"Please proceed, have a nice evening Josh",

"Thanks, you too", said Phipps.

He crossed the shagpile, through the gate onto the marble floor, down the hall to the lift at the end, watched at every step by a moving camera. At the lift, there were no buttons, just a speaker and microphone in the wall.

"Warden Joshua Phipps, shift number 15,894 complete, permission to leave the facility?",

"We've been expecting you Mr Bond" said the voice of Randy Huber, the lift security guard, who had been making the same joke for nearly all of Phipps' shifts.

He was a big James Bond fan, watching all the old classics, despite most other people not understanding the joke about a fictitious spy who had been popular 200 years before.

"On my way up".

A few moments later the lift doors opened, Phipps stepped in beside Herber and they both made their way to ground level. As is usually the case in lifts, neither man spoke.

7

Herber handed Phipps the clipboard, Phipps signed and at once the doors opened. The foyer at the ground floor of the building was always busy with yet more security guards but apart from that, looking much like any other foyer in any other office building with marble floors, marble walls and big glass doors to the world outside. Phipps made his way to the large reception desk,

"Warden Joshua Phipps, shift number 15,894 complete, permission to leave the facility?"

One more signature and at precisely 6:00pm and 11 seconds, Phipps pushed open the glass door to the sidewalk beyond.

The subway, one block south, took no time, and five stops later Phipps was in his neighbourhood. A quick visit to the supermarket and he was headed back home to his apartment.

He unlocked the door, stepped inside, and tossed his keys, as he always did, in the key tray on the side table, before heading to the kitchen to drop his groceries. The kitchen was a mess, dirty plates and cutlery pilled precariously high in the sink; he had not felt much like doing even the most basic things since it had happened. After his supper, a simple affair, he moved to the lounge, picked up the picture, slumped in his chair, and stared. Staring back from the photograph was a beautiful girl, not more than seven, thick long curly auburn hair, green eyes and a toothless, endless, grin. Phipps welled up and the tears rolled down his cheeks as they had many times before.

2
GREEN RIVERS

The entire Green River 5 facility was a state-of-the-art marvel. The plans for any building were created in the normal way with detailed drawings of every aspect using computer aided design, a 3D printer did the rest. Every plug socket, wire, shower head TV, radio, camera, heating, and air conditioning system, absolutely everything was made miniature to the very last detail. Green River 5 took just over three weeks to build using a 3D printer and the Vegas style Palomino Beach Resort, Spa Hotel and Golf Course took just six, using three printers. Technology, as always, was moving at the speed of light. The shrink beams flicked on every few minutes, like strobe lighting, keeping inmates just the right amount shrunk, and all the walls of the prisons were coated in a special paint, so they didn't shrink along with inmates. The only shrunk things in Green River 5, or elsewhere for that matter, were the people.

The facility sat right in the centre of a circular base, about the same size as a dinner plate, with a glass dome sealing it all in. At opposite sides of each dome were two pipes, one carrying power, air, water, and the feed for a shrink beam, and the other to pipe waste out. A 6ft man would stand just 3mm tall inside the dome, just about visible to the naked eye. The dome was made of thick glass which magnified the activities of the inhabitants for onlookers such as Phipps and the like. Inmates looking out of the dome, during their yard exercise breaks, would see only misty shadows of wardens pacing their offices. There were very few guards inside the domes as there was rarely any trouble but, if something did break out between the inmates, sleeping gas would be pumped in and the offenders removed, to wake up in solitary. As with any prison, since prisons were invented, contraband could be, and was, smuggled into Green River 5. Many illicit materials found their way through the food supply. To put things into perspective, a small pea would be about twice the height of a 6ft man and peas were rolled in weekly!

Jack had served six years of his lifetime incarceration in the east wing of Green River 5, and he had been very busy. In the first few months Jack had befriended Willy G Patterson, who was responsible for seeing in food deliveries, preparation, and the canteen servery. In turn, Willy G had a cousin on the outside, Herb, who worked for Smallz, a catering firm, with a near monopoly on food provision for prisons and some of the larger resorts. The P Train, as it became known, was a popular smuggling vehicle for almost anything that would fit inside a pea.

Conjugal rights were still allowed for most prisoners, and

the wives, husbands and partners of inmates were able to visit their loved ones monthly, and this is how the big stuff got smuggled in. A visitor would arrive at the jail, and all jewellery items, broaches, watches etc. would be removed along with clothing, but never undergarments. Wives, husbands and partners would be shrunk for a two-hour visit in private, and all manner of items were cleverly sewn into their underwear. Need a length of copper cable, some carbon fibre, maybe fibre optic, metals, plastic, all possible because even before they were shrunk, these items were tiny. During the visit items would be passed on and hidden in miniature before they grew back to their original size shielded from the shrink beams. It was a constant source of amazement to the residents of the east wing that the guards on the outside didn't catch on to this ruse, but shrunk incarceration was in its infancy, loopholes not yet closed, and after all, those on the outside were seeing things from a very different perspective.

It was under these conditions that Jack, and his team began to build. Their first hurdle was to create a space away from the prying eyes of Warden Phipps, yet every single room had at least one camera and sometimes more. The time travelling inmates of the east wing numbered 12 in total, eight men and four women. It was the only wing in any facility in the whole of the US that housed both men and women. The group fell into three categories: military, scientists, and the uber wealthy. Military because they were the original government approved travellers, trained in the past. The scientists were those who understood how the whole thing worked, and the uber wealthy because they could afford the vast costs associated with time travel. All were extremely bright, the top of their respective fields, but one in particular, Professor Friedrich Von Shultz - or Freddie as he was affectionately known – was the cleverest of all and completely insane.

3
PROFESSOR FRIEDRICH VON SHULTZ

Freddie had a long-held view that Adolf Hitler carried out all those atrocities because he was not loved and cared for properly as a child, so, together with his wife Hilda, hatched a plan to go back in time to kidnap Hitler and bring him up as their own. The plan was of course foiled, Freddie ended up in Green River 5, Hilda was committed to a sanitorium in 1893, and the rest is history.

Freddie was straight out of central casting in appearance as a mad professor. He stood about 5'8" tall, of slight build, with a balding head of grey curly hair. He always looked as if he had just awoken from a restless night's sleep and had not had the thought to use a comb, in fact, it was fair assumption that he didn't even own one.

Freddie was tasked with working out how the group could build what they wanted to without being seen by the ever-present CCTV cameras. The indoor gym facility on the second floor of the east wing was chosen. It was marked out as a basketball court and was dedicated to the east wing inmates only. The shrink beam in that room had a motion sensor, one camera at one end of the court captured the entire vastness of the room and the professors' solution was beautiful in its simplicity. He theorised that a giant mirror correctly angled at exactly the centre of the court would show an image of the entire court on camera whilst dividing the room completely in half.

The mirror trick had been used by magicians for centuries to conceal flowers, birds, rabbits even people in their illusions and it meant that the work of Jack and his crew could be carried out behind the mirror unseen, genius.

Calculations were made, checked, rechecked and checked again, all helped by the absolute precision in dimensions to millionths of a micron of the 3D printer that made Green River 5 in the first place. There were no wobbly side lines here, no skewwhiff walls, it was all precision stuff. And so it came to pass that a highly polished plastic mirror, fashioned as a classy underwear label, and measuring 21mm by 8mm, was smuggled into prison without so much as a glance from the guards who were pretending not to look at the dozen or so women standing in their underwear. The mirror was fixed in exactly the right place at exactly the right angle and would in a few hours begin to grow back to full size. Sure enough, it worked perfectly. It meant that if a guard came to check the sports hall, which happened on rare occasion, he would see an empty space. If he walked too far into the room, which he had never done yet, he would start to see a mirror image of himself and the game would be up, but it was a risk the crew were prepared to take.

After that, spirits on the east wing ran high, after all, if they could smuggle in a mirror equivalent of 18 feet tall and 36 feet wide, what couldn't they do without the right planning. Work began in earnest and before long, the makeshift workshop, hidden behind a magician's mirror, was nearly half filled with all manner of equipment. There were solar panels, cables, lots of thin strands of carbon fibre, two large bulbous golden reflective glass lenses, lightweight sailing fabric, sheets of aluminium, long lengths of spider web and much more. Led by Freddie, the two other scientists worked tirelessly on blueprints, often arguing but always making progress. The military group worked in shifts to piece together a machine, the like of which had never been designed, let alone built before. In a tiny corner of a tiny room in a tiny building, no bigger than a large pat of butter, under a glass dome in an office on the 13th floor of a nondescript, heavily guarded, building somewhere in New York, something was happening that might possibly change the course of history forever.

4
JOSHUA PHIPPS

Warden Phipps was a large man, he stood just over 6 feet tall and in his younger days might have been described as athletic, but now was nearly as wide as he was tall. He always wore a three piece pinstriped suit, shirt and tie, with an old fashioned pocket watch which had been handed down through his family. His features were rounded due to his overall size with a full curly mop of mousy unkempt hair. He also wore a moustache, something his wife, long departed, had expressed a liking for. On the odd occasion he gave it a trim in the mirror, he would talk to her, beyond the grave, about whatever was on his mind at that particular time.

He generally left his apartment around 8:30am each morning, heading to the local deli on the corner of his block for breakfast. Just as most other folks were leaving by 8:45am, he was generally the only customer left, Phipps liked it that way.

"Morning Josh," said Mary brightly as she slid a coffee under Phipps' nose.

"Morning Mary," grunted Phipps, slipping into a booth without looking up from his news tablet.

"Usual?" she said and without waiting for an answer, turned and headed away.

"Usual for Josh Bert" she shouted in the general direction of the kitchen.

Phipps always had the usual, and today was no different. Breakfast was served and eaten in silence. Phipps then pulled a couple of credits from his pocket, slipped them on the table and made for the door.

"Time," said Mary.

"What?" replied Phipps.

"Time, it gets easier with time. I remember when Chuck, I mean, I know it's not the same but," her voice lowered to a whisper, and she bowed her head. *"Oh, it doesn't matter, same time tomorrow?"*

Phipps nodded, looked down at his shoes, pulled at the door and headed to work.

He reached the office at around 9:34am and entered the building through a different door to the one he had exited the night before. A camera filmed his entry and tracked him to reception where he met a man with no uniform, sitting in front of him.

"Mr Phipps, good morning, you are booked for shift 16,025, please

sign here."

Phipps didn't recognise the man, he never did, these guards, always in plain clothes, were on rotation, and although he never knew their names, they always knew his.

"Please proceed".

Phipps passed through reception and headed to the first of many doors. A loud buzz sounded, and he entered a chamber, with a second door just beyond the first. He approached another camera, and the door clicked behind him before another buzzer sounded and he passed through, only to be greeted by more security.

"You know the drill," said the guard.

Yet another stranger, but this time in uniform. Phipps set down his briefcase and flask, held out his hands, palms up, then lifted his arms above his head slowly, whilst the guard passed a metal detecting wand over him, frisking at every bleep the machine made.

"Keys," said the guard and Phipps obeyed, taking the apartment keys from his pocket.

The guard repeated the sweep, nodded, and pointed to the next door. Another buzz and he was through, this time to face another guard, and another signature, before reaching the final door before the lift. The door buzzed open to a slightly larger room, and this time he was met by three guards.

"Number two today Mr Phipps," said the guard sitting at desk two.

Thank goodness not three, thought Phipps, that guy always riffled his briefcase and upset its ordered contents. Phipps approached the desk, set his briefcase and flask down, opened the case, span it around, and the guard peered in.

"Ok," he said.

Phipps snapped the briefcase closed, headed towards the lift as the doors opened automatically, sending him off to the 13th floor.

"8 Bells," said Harry Williams as Phipps entered the office.

"8 Bells," mumbled Phipps.

"Hey Josh, Stella was wondering if you'd like to come over next time we're not on rotation, she'll do ribs, you said you liked those?"

"I do," said Phipps.

"Then its settled." Williams paused for a moment, as if to find the right words,

"It will get easier, it takes time," he touched Phipps' arm as he passed him on his way out.

Williams turned back, *"Oh yeah, east wing, they need to be getting more exercise, only three in the yard again on my shift. See you tomorrow".*

"Tomorrow," repeated Phipps as the door closed behind him. Time, he thought, how much time, how long before he started to feel even the slightest bit better? Again, he fought back the tears.

5
CONSTRUCTION

It was all hands to the pump on the east wing and had been for many months. The entire crew were working every hour they could on the machine, which was slowly taking shape. It looked like a very large table supported by six bent carbon fibre legs. The legs were black, and the odd shaped tabletop was silver, slanting from front to back in three distinct sections of different sizes. The smallest was at the front of the machine, whilst a larger one made up the middle, followed by the largest section at the rear. There were four inmates working on top fixing cables, wires and boxes of various sizes and each time they moved up and down the structure, the legs bowed very slightly like springs. Below the tabletop, two more were working to fit four cameras to the underside. At the front, laying on the floor were two large bulbous, golden reflective glass lenses and lent against the wall behind them, two giant opalescent structures that looked rather like wind surfing sails, accompanied by carbon fibre rib supports. The whole structure looked a bit cobbled together, wires hung over the edges of the table, boxes attached to the tabletop had more wires and odd shaped rods, created for heaven knows what, pointing skywards. Compared to the precise lines of its surroundings, this thing looked very much like a giant science project, created by a small child during the holidays, using everything to hand whether required or not. Furthermore, Jack and one or two others on the east wing knew, even if they finished this project, there was one very important component missing, and they had absolutely no idea how they were going to get it.

6
PHIPPS MEETS PALMER

Phipps stared into the dome of Green River 5 and at the sectioned off exercise yard of the east wing, three inmates were standing together talking. He moved back to his desk, pressed some buttons and was immediately viewing the east wing on one screen. The images here were all too small for proper scrutiny so he flicked through the cells and the other rooms one by one. He paused at the sports hall, nobody there. Another button and the communications channel opened to the east wing.

"Palmer to the communications room, five minutes," barked Phipps, as he watched all cameras to the east wing on one screen again.

He witnessed a hive of activity amongst the dozen inmates, making their way in and out of rooms, passing each other. How many could he see, eight or was it 10, no 12, but where was Palmer? He stood up and walked over to the dome to see the three inmates previously in the yard, re-entering the prison through the door to the exercise yard. Phipps walked back to his desk, flicked the channel to the east wing communication room and waited. The communication room was set up rather like a police interview room with one chair, and one desk which faced a camera on the opposite wall. Precisely five minutes after Phipps had called for Palmer, he entered the communications room and sat on the chair behind the desk.

"We've been noticing that not many of your number are using the exercise yard of late, why's that, you know the rules?"

Palmer thought for a moment,

"Well, the Professor still has a dodgy knee, Mrs Braithwaite doesn't get around much anyway, Millie has had an upset stomach but, the rest of us are doing our quota."

Phipps quickly flicked through the rooms once more, two inmates in cells doing press ups, two at the centre of the sports hall, holding hands doing squats, and another three just entering the yard.

"OK," said Phipps *"more yard exercise, the fresh air will do you all good."*

"The air's the same wherever you are in here", said Palmer.

Phipps smiled, although Palmer couldn't see him.

"Ok, that's all, you can go", said Phipps.

Palmer got up to leave, but stopped,

23

"We were all very sorry to hear about the sad news, it's a shame this whole thing has been outlawed, it could have been very…"

"Enough," shouted Phipps interrupting, *"get out".*

He flicked off the communications room monitor, and sat, breathing heavily as he looked at the blank screen, trying to regain his composure. That evening back at the apartment, Phipps stared for longer than ever at the picture of dear sweet Lucy. He had barely slept since it happened, and that night, he didn't sleep a wink.

7

BAD NEWS TRAVELS FAST

Palmer and the crew had heard about the accident, a hit and run a few weeks before, from Danny Maguire, the only guard on the east wing. Guards patrolling Green River 5, and all the other prisons in the system, lived in, shrunk like the prisoners, on one-year contracts and Danny was on his fourth tour. The nature of the work meant that most guards did not have wives, husbands or partners and were generally quite young. The work was well paid; Danny was saving for a deposit for his first house but, the main reason for him rolling into year four was that he was sweet on Millie Salzburg, one of the 12 inmates on east wing. Danny relished every opportunity to speak to Millie and it became her main job to delay or divert Danny whenever the need arose. Millie liked Danny too, not quite in the same way but, he was a nice lad. Danny would spend a good deal of time thinking about what he might say to Millie next. If she expressed even the slightest interest in anything, he would work hard at researching that particular topic, so he could speak to her about it the next time they met. Danny spent a lot of time researching in his guard room apartment. The east wing was originally designed to take up to 250 inmates, so Danny had less to do than most, but he was always busy researching at his computer or doing the rounds.

That lunchtime, Millie bumped into Danny in the corridor,

"Hey Danny boy, how's it going?" she said, looking at him in that way she did.

"Oh, I'm ok Millie, I wish I could say the same for Warden Phipps".

Danny went on to tell Millie about Lucy, Phipps' granddaughter, who was tragically mowed down on the pavement. The joyrider, a teenager, was also killed instantly. Apparently, Phipps had seen the whole thing as he was returning from buying Lucy an ice cream across the road from the park. Danny and Millie both stood, heads bowed, for as long as circumstances would allow, before heading off in opposite directions, Millie to go tell the crew and Danny, to his room, to research joyriding and anything else he thought might interest Millie the next time they met.

8
THE FLYING MACHINE

Apart from the most important component, the machine was nearly complete. All that was left was the shell, the outer casing, just like the chassis of car. This was a problem, it needed to be a complete unit made of carbon fibre, and it needed to fit the base precisely. It required the precision of a 3D printer. The crew set about hatching a plan. Blueprints for the shell had been drawn by the Professor sometime earlier but they were extremely detailed and, therefore, quite large. The plans were drawn on four sheets of standard draftsman's paper, which, on the outside, measured 2ft wide by 1.5ft tall each. Of course, on the inside, they were a fraction of this size but, they couldn't be smuggled out in underwear, and besides, they had only ever used this method to smuggle things in. Thoughts turned to the food supply. Apart from the peas and a few other items, many food stuffs were delivered to the prison in long strips, just like a sausage roll is made, only much longer. Apple pie, a favourite with the inmates, would have its pastry on the outside with the filling in the middle. Willie G, in the canteen, gave half the inmates on the west wing food poisoning by contaminating the apple pie. Herb at Smallz was contacted, and it was arranged for samples to be sent back directly for analysis, and that's how the blueprints made it out, rolled up neatly in the apple pie pastry. Herb also obliged by setting up a spot check system whereby samples, selected by Willie G, would be periodically sent back, providing a useful communication channel to the outside. The chassis was delivered shortly afterwards, sewn onto the front of a pair of knickers, precision built by a 3D printer using the Professors exacting plans and of course, it fitted perfectly. The chassis also had the effect of smartening up the whole appearance of their creation.

The two large bulbous, golden reflective glass lenses were fitted to the front of the structure, where two holes in the chassis had been provided, and the only items, not yet fitted, were the two giant opalescent wind surfing sails that still lent against the wall. At the top of the machine were two massive metal knuckles much like you might see on the roof of a helicopter, at the centre, to secure the blades. Even without wings, it was clear to the untrained eye, the crew had managed to build a flying machine, and not just any flying machine, this aircraft looked exactly like a giant housefly.

"Let's test the engines," said the professor.

"Are you sure Freddie," said Jack, *"What about the noise?"*.

"It will be quiet without the wings," said the professor reassuringly,

"Ok then,"

and in a flash Jack had climbed into the cockpit, strapped himself in and positioned his finger over a large red button, with the word START stamped on it. The engines immediately whirred into life and Freddie was right, it was quiet, little more than the sound of a large office fan, Jack was impressed. The craft bounced gently up and down on its six carbon fibre legs and the knuckles on the roof were just a blur to the naked eye, such was the speed at which they were moving. Jack cut the engines, jumped out, walked over to the professor, and hugged him.

"We did it, we did it, Freddie! Let's go and tell the others".

"We did," said the professor, *"but you know we weren't the first".*

Jack looked puzzled,

"I'll tell you later," replied the professor, and off they went to share the news.

That day, and the weeks and months that followed, proved good for the east wing. The craft was continually modified, and the professor managed to improve the estimated flying time by a further 30 minutes. The massive wings were fitted, even the carbon fibre moulded seats, six in all, were given padded upholstery but, it had never actually been flown. The crew endlessly discussed how they might test the aircraft within the confines of the sports hall without getting caught, but each scenario discussed threw up too many imponderables, and too many risks.

9
YES OR NO

Phipps sat behind the desk in his office, a world away in his own thoughts, constantly weighing his options, going over and over and coming right back to the start. Occasionally leaning in towards the bank of buttons in front of him, but at the last minute, withdrawing back into his thoughts. It had been like this all morning and well into the afternoon when finally, he broke.

"Palmer to the communications room, five minutes".

This was both the longest and the shortest five minutes, in a way that only time can be; it's all relative. Phipps bit his nails, moved nervously on the office swivel chair, never comfortable, never at ease, but instead, a cocktail of excitement and nerves. It wouldn't hurt to ask, he thought over and over, it's not a crime to ask, to see what this guy says. Then all at once and, also after an eternity, the communications room door opened, Jack walked in and took the seat.

"How are you doing down there?" said Phipps.

"I'd rather be elsewhere," replied Palmer.

There was a pause, a long pause, and then,

"The last time we met, you spoke of something you shouldn't have known about in there," said Phipps.

"I don't remember how I heard," replied Jack,

"I don't care about that," snapped Phipps, cutting him short.

He continued,

"It can only have been Maguire and I don't care about that," regaining his composure. *"I want to know what you meant by, 'if only', blah blah blah?"*

After another long pause, Jack cleared his throat and began,

"It happened three weeks ago, right?"

Phipps nodded, but Jack couldn't see him, another pause,

"Yes," said Phipps, his voice breaking slightly.

"Lucy was young, the driver of the car also died, and you saw the whole thing?" said Jack.

"Yes that's all correct," said Phipps almost whispering now.

"Were there any other witnesses, it's important?"

"Other children, in the park," said Phipps.

"Any adults, it's important?" said Jack.

"I don't think so, why?" replied Phipps.

"Because children are less likely to have a residual memory scar from such an incident," said Jack.

"Meaning?" enquired Phipps.

"Meaning it might have been possible to change the past without too much of a tremor in the present. Child witnesses, and the length of time since it happened is relatively short,"

Jack sensed the tide of the conversation was moving in his favour.

"Take me back to the very beginning and tell me everything, don't miss out a single detail, no matter how small and insignificant it may seem".

For the next 40 minutes that's exactly what Phipps did, fighting his pain all the way, the only consolation, he thought, was that Palmer could not see the tears springing from his eyes, down his cheeks, and onto his shirt.

Jack left the communications room and went directly to Millie, his closest confident. Millie was also ex-military, a pilot, trained in time travel, and an all-round solid girl. She could be relied upon in a fix and Jack trusted her implicitly. Millie stood just 5'8" tall, she was very fit with a slight frame and long dark hair and pretty features, out of her prison uniform she would have scrubbed up very well. Millie was inside for jumping back in time for a wealthy guy, who suspected his wife had cheated. An easy job on paper, but things went wrong and here she was. The only two things she knew for sure was that the wife hadn't done it, and the husband gave Millie up when, in her opinion, he didn't need to. Both Millie and the husband, Bob Gosling, were both sent to the east wing and, needless to say, they did everything they could to avoid each other.

"So, do you think Phipps will do it?" said Millie,

"I really don't know," replied Jack, *"but we don't have another plan, and this is the last piece of the jigsaw. I didn't go into detail exactly, but he knows what we need so all we can do now is wait and see. One thing's for sure, he'll have to make his mind up soon. It's been three weeks since the accident, and we can't afford to wait much longer if we're to have any chance, we're pushing it as it is."*

They sat in silence for a moment, it was a long shot, but better than no shot at all.

"Don't say anything to the others yet, I don't want to get their hopes up," said Jack.

"Roger that," said Millie.

****

Phipps sat in his apartment, staring at Lucy, Lucy staring back from the photograph. His emotions were mixed, on the one hand, the slightest whisp of hope, on the other, doing something that went against every principle he had held dear since as long as he could remember. If Palmer messed this up, he'd go to jail, and they would throw away the key. It had been three weeks since the incident and just over a week since the funeral. His daughter had barely spoken to him afterwards. He thought, in fact he knew, that she somehow blamed him. If Lucy wasn't visiting him, this would never have happened. The possibility, however remote, of the whole thing being extinguished and everything going back to how it was before, was extremely appealing. Nobody expected him to go back to work so soon but what was he supposed to do, sit around the apartment moping. His boss tried to dissuade him, but he insisted, and they relented. He knew he faced the biggest decision he had ever faced in his life, and he couldn't decide which way to go.

****

"What did you mean Freddie when you said we were not the first?" asked Jack in front of the others, in the canteen.

"We are not the first prisoners to build a flying machine in a prison under the noses of the guards," said the professor.

"What?" said Millie disbelievingly, as the others, also sceptical, looked in his direction.

"Has this got anything to do with Hitler?" said Elspeth Braithwaite.

"No, well yes." Everyone groaned.

"No not directly, but yes because it happened in the second world war, which happened because Hitler invaded Poland, and the British got involved, and people died, and prisoners were taken".

All were now starting to get interested in the story. The professor was mad, everyone would agree on that, but he did know his onions when it came to anything to do with Hitler and therefore, the second world war.

"There was a castle in Germany, in a town called Colditz, in the Leipzig district of Saxony. The castle was used to house prisoners of war, initially from Belgium, France, Poland, the Netherlands, and Canada and eventually only the British," said Freddie. *"The castle was labelled escape proof by the Germans, there were 174 attempts and 32 men actually escaped to freedom, half from within the castles walls".*

"And the flying machine?" questioned Millie.

"Yes, I was getting to that", said the professor. *"In the eaves of the castle roof, prisoners constructed a fully functional glider, which was designed to carry two men off the roof and across the River Mulde, 60 metres below".*

"And?" said Millie, *"did they escape to freedom?"*

"No," said the professor, and everyone groaned.

"The flight never took place because the Americans arrived and liberated the castle."

"Never flown," said Millie, *"that sounds familiar"* and they all laughed nervously.

Within seconds, Danny Maguire approached them,

"What's all this fun about?" Millie gave him one of her looks,

"Freddie is talking about Hitler again," they all laughed.

Danny thought how lucky he was looking after this lot compared to his colleagues on the other wings and the other prisons. He walked back to his rooms to research Hitler a bit just in case it came up in conversation with Millie.

****

Once again, Phipps didn't sleep a wink, and that morning he sat alone in the deli, no closer to a decision than he had been since the conversation the day before with Jack Palmer. Mary approached with his coffee.

"Morning Josh",

"Morning Mary".

"Sorry about yesterday," said Mary, *"It's just we're all terribly sad, and we want to help you, life can be so cruel sometimes and for no good reason".*

"Don't worry," said Phipps, *"I know you all mean well".*

"Usual for Josh," shouted Mary over her shoulder.

"So young," said Mary, *"her whole life in front of her, it should all have been so different."*

Mary turned and walked away. Should have been so different, thought Phipps, could be so different, yes it could, it could be different. Phipps got up from the booth with purpose and headed for the door. Mary watched as he left, she had upset him again she thought, and vowed to try to keep her mouth shut in future. Phipps arrived at his office a full 30 minutes early that morning and waited on the sidewalk wondering what Palmer would have to say when they spoke. Time slowed down but eventually Phipps found himself in his office for the hand over, this time with Walter P Courage.

"Warden Phipps, the printouts are on the desk, nothing in the incident log, east wing inmates were exercising more than over the last few weeks",

"Thank you, Warden Courage," said Phipps and they parted company.

Phipps drew little comfort from the newly found exercise regime in the east wing.

10
LANTHANEODINIUM

A few years earlier, prior to work commencing on the aircraft, and just after their incarceration, the crew were discussing time travel machines. These machines were very rare, and distribution strictly controlled by governments around the world. There were two types, the handheld TTm1, about the size of a bar of soap, which was ideal for one or two travellers on a mission. This was most used in the early days of time travel, these machines were quite common, and a few found their way onto the black market and changed hands for many millions. The inmates in the east wing were all very familiar with these machines. Then there was a larger machine, developed in Germany, and licenced by Bayer Zeit Losungen, a subsidiary of a much larger electronics company, which allowed for many travellers and tonnes of equipment. This machine, The Bayze, a state of the art, technological masterpiece, was about the size of two standard house bricks, and there were seven known to be in existence. All time machines were extremely heavy, due to a recently discovered Rare Earth known as Lanthaneodinium, an essential element which made time travel possible. Lanthaneodinium had a specific gravity of 38.2, over twice the weight of lead or gold. A TTm1 weighed in at four kilos and The Bayze, amazing given its size, a staggering 26 kilos. All time machines were very simple to operate and worked on two principles, where and when, with separate readouts for each. The where was calculated using longitude and latitude, to many decimal places, to ensure pinpoint accuracy and, the when, a digital clock that would operate to one tenth of a second. If you wanted to return to 11:58am on the 22nd of May 1979, the dial would be turned until the display showed 001979.05.22.11.58.00.00. In the same vein, depressing the dial would send you back. The Americans and British quote their days and months in different order, which caused a few problems early on, but these were resolved by ensuring you couldn't operate the dial until you had stated your preference.

Elspeth Braithwaite was the wife of the departed Harold Braithwaite, an energy tycoon, who amongst many other things, owned a Lanthaneodinium mine, the only one in existence, situated on the border between Eritrea and Ethiopia. Elspeth was here because Harold had been discovered selling Lanthaneodinium to the Saudis, without the proper licences. Harold never made it to trial, due to a fatal heart attack caused by stress, but after his death all eyes focused on Elspeth. It was a widely held view, and certainly by the crew of the east wing, that Elspeth was innocent, and if Harold had made the trial he would be here, and she would still be a free woman. The Braithwaite's were an extraordinarily wealthy couple and with no children, Elspeth used to do the charity circuit giving many millions to good causes, particularly children's causes, but all that wealth and all that charity did not help Elspeth to stay out of jail. She was 5'6" tall, about a size 16 with a handsome happy face and dyed blonde hair. Elspeth was like a kindly maiden aunt, the one you could confide in regarding delicate matters, she was conversational in many languages including Urdu, had a doctorate in psychology from Yale and about as down to earth a person as you could wish to meet. Everyone liked Elspeth. The family was old money and she had been brought up to be comfortable with that, and after all she was innocent, right? That's what they thought, until the day when they were all discussing time machines.

Elspeth joined Jack and Millie in the exercise yard, the crew had been having as many meetings as possible there since Phipps' comments a day or so earlier. They walked together around the perimeter, a large shadow from beyond the glass dome peered in. Jack wondered if it were Phipps and, if so, what he had decided, there was no way of telling.

"Remember the early days?" said Jack, *"we'd all been in a short while and we were weighing our options".*

"We've all been doing that since the start, Honey" said Elspeth,

"And ever since" chipped in Millie.

"No, the time machine conversations," said Jack helpfully,

"plenty of those too honey," said Elspeth.

"The Bayze," said Jack finally,

"Oh, The Bayze, still there I would guess unless Brandy dug it up"

she chuckled.

Brandy was Elspeth's brown Labrador, she loved and missed him dearly.

"We need it, at least I think we might need it, it's a long shot, a very long shot but, there's a chance," said Jack quickly.

"Wow," said Elspeth in amazement, *"Well I'm sure it's still there in the garden where Harold left it, god rest his soul."*

Elspeth paused for a moment, her memories drifting back to a life with Brandy and Harold. Harold had his heart attack directly after burying The Bayze in the garden.

"Yup, still there," she whispered.

Jack filled Elspeth in on the conversation so far with Phipps, and Elspeth gave as much detail as she could regarding the whereabouts of the machine, and the help he would need. Jack asked Elspeth not to mention it to the others, and she agreed, as they knew she would.

11
THE DECISION

Phipps headed back to his desk, as the three inmates in green River 5 returned inside. In for a penny, in for a pound, he thought and hit the communications button. His heart was pounding, the cocktail of fear and excitement running through his veins once more.

"Palmer to the communications room, five minutes".

Jack was just getting back into the facility with Millie and Elspeth when he heard the call come over the intercom.

"Here goes," he said,

"Good luck" said both Elspeth and Millie in unison.

They smiled, and Jack smiled too as he turned and made his way to the communication room to take his seat. Jack sat there for a few minutes, and whilst waiting, wondered what

Warden Phipps must look like. Phipps watched Jack Palmer in detail for those few minutes. He stood 6'3" tall, with broad shoulders, he was well built, due to a strict exercise regime inside, although he had always been in good shape. He had short dark hair parted at one side and handsome features with a chiseled jaw, the type of man you might see in an aftershave advert.

Phipps flicked the comms switch.

"What guarantees do I have?"

Jack paused, cleared his throat, then paused some more,

"None," he said finally.

"You're not selling this", said Phipps.

Another pause,

"You want a guarantee, I'll give you a guarantee," said Jack. *"If you don't do this, nothing changes, and if you do, you might not like the changes, we've all got a lot to lose here."*

"I've got more to lose than you", said Phipps.

"And a damn sight more to gain" interjected Jack. *"If you don't want to go ahead, just say, we are wasting time, and we have precious little of that left Warden"*.

Phipps, thought for a moment,

"OK what do I need to do?"

Jack then proceeded to go through every detail of the plan as he saw it, careful not to mention the elements Phipps did

43

not need to know about, including the conjugal visits, the pea train, the giant fly in the sports hall, but he did provide a list of vital information including several visits to premises across the city.

"Dog biscuits?" asked Phipps, *"what the hell, are you kidding me?"*

"Look," said Jack, *"all will become clear, if you want the best chance here, you need to follow the instructions to the letter".*

Jack told Phipps the minimum of information, as he made each stop on his journey around the city, more would unfold.

"The shrink is down to you," said Jack, *"are we clear on that?"*

"We are clear," said Phipps,

"How will you manage it?" asked Jack.

"That's down to me, and frankly you've got a nerve asking, when I'm to travel halfway across town for dog biscuits!"

Jack grinned and Phipps grinned too, but Jack didn't see him. The stage was set.

Millie waited patiently for Jack to finish his meeting with Phipps. Whilst sitting there she thought the time had come to ask Jack why he ended up in here. She knew everybody else's story, and if this whole thing was to work, she would need to know his.

"And?" she said, as Jack approached.

"All set," he replied, *"it's in the lap of the gods now".*

"Good, now it's time you and I had a chat".

They both headed for the canteen and sat apart from the group. Elspeth was making her way to join them, when Millie discreetly shook her head, and Elspeth peeled off to another table. Jack knew this day would come and he knew it would be Millie sitting in front of him when he told his story. Jack went right back to the beginning, when he, and his twin brother James, were just six years old. He was in the yard, it was blowing a gale, and dust was in the air all around him. A shot rang out, and he ran back inside to find his mother lying dead, in a pool of blood, on the kitchen floor, a revolver beside her, and his father driving away down the long road from the farm, dust billowing from the track behind him. Jack told Millie that the police caught up with his father in town, he was arrested, he confessed, and he got the chair. Jack had travelled back to that day, something he needed to see, something went wrong, as it often does when you meddle with the past, and he ended up here.

"But what did you need to see?" said Millie,

"That's enough for one day," said Jack. *"Come on, we've got plenty to do, and we don't have much time".*

They both got up and headed for the sports hall.

12
THE JOURNEY

Phipps perused the list he had scribbled whilst talking to Palmer. *"Dog biscuits,"* he mumbled, before heading for the subway and on to the first of many visits that night, carrying an empty briefcase, the contents of which had been removed at his apartment earlier that evening. First stop, Hanks Printer Repair, a dingy shop with a flickering neon in the window. Phipps entered, a bell above the door rang and an Indian man, wearing a turban, appeared from the back of the shop.

"I was just…" Phipps started,

"I know, said the man, *"let's see it".*

Phipps placed the empty briefcase on the counter,

"And the contents?" said the man,

"I was told to empty,"

"I know," said the man interrupting again.

"Did you take photographs of the contents" speaking as if he were talking to a child.

"Yes," said Phipps, reaching inside his pocket for his phone.

"Email," said the man, pointing to a dirty old display card on the counter, with an email address on it.

Phipps obliged and sent on the pictures he had taken from his phone.

"Hold on," said the man, as he moved to a computer screen behind the counter, *"Not exactly Annie Liebowitz are we!"*

The man inspected the photographs,

"They will do I suppose, I'll need a few hours".

"Do I get a receipt?" asked Phipps,

"No," said the man,

"What if you are not here when I come back?" said Phipps,

"I'm always here," said the man,

and with that, he returned to the back of the shop, leaving Phipps standing at the counter. Phipps turned and left, with a plan to return.

The clock was ticking, it was now just 13 hours before Phipps was due back on duty and Millie, Elspeth and Jack would know for sure if the first part of the plan had been successful. It was all systems go and the others in the crew felt a sense of urgency in the air.

"Anything I should know Jack?" asked the professor,

"Not yet Freddie," said Jack, *"But, I'll be sure to tell you, let's just treat this exercise as a drill and I'll say more when I can."*

The professor nodded and continued with his work. Jack climbed into the aircraft cockpit and sat next to Millie, who was checking dials in the co-pilots seat.

"Hey Millie, you'll need to go down there just before midnight and keep him busy for a further 10 minutes, are you ready, can you do that?"

Millie nodded.

"It's going to be noisy, but he must under no circumstances be allowed to come in here, do you understand?"

Millie nodded again, pretending to busy herself by flicking pages on the notes she had in her lap.

"Millie," said Jack loudly.

"Yes Jack, I get it, and I will do everything I need to do to, everything!" she said as her eyes levelled on Jack. *"Now, get on with your job, and leave me to do mine, ok?".*

"Ok," said Jack as he got up to leave. He turned back to face Millie,

"You know, use your judgement",

"Enough," said Millie smiling, *"It's all under control".*

****

48

Phipps arrived at Posh Pouch, in Manhattan.

"Just in time," said the old lady assistant, dressed in a pink woollen Chanel suit with white piping and a peroxide blonde set. *"We were just closing; you'll have to be quick".*

It was 10:00pm and Phipps was running late.

"Can I have a packet of Kobe beef and truffle doggy chew biscuits please?",

"Oh who's the lucky fella, or bitch?" said the lady.

"They're for my dog",

"I know silly," she said, *"What's their name?",*

"Erm, erm, Jack," spluttered Phipps.

"Jack ha, I love it, well Jack's going to love these", she said as she reached below the counter and passed Phipps the treats.

"That's 87 credits please".

Jeez thought Phipps but he paid, picked up the goods and was soon gone in the back of a yellow taxicab he hailed outside. There were no subway stations where he was going.

****

Millie headed to find Danny; he was in the canteen watching the staff clean up the kitchen.

"Hey Danny",

"Hi Millie, did you know that joy riding accidents have decreased year on year for the last four years, so when you look at it that way, Warden

Phipps' granddaughter was especially unlucky".

Millie looked quizzically at him.

"Danny, I was wondering if you fancied a chat?",

"Sure," said Danny, *"Let me just get this lot out of the wing,"* he said pointing at the kitchen staff, *"And then I've then got a bit of time before my rounds",*

"Great," said Millie.

Behind the mirror in the sports hall there was a hive of activity. Spiders' web had been attached to all six legs of the craft and secured with weights to the basketball floor. The professor, together with the other scientists, were in a huddle, looking at plans, two inmates sat on top, applying grease to the huge metal knuckles attached to the wings. Jack sat in the cockpit, strapped in, tapping each of the dials one by one. The other inmates, stood at various points in the east wing keeping a look out.

****

Phipps, travelled at speed in the back of the yellow taxicab, headed for Connecticut. It was fast approaching midnight and Phipps was worried, he was running late. The enormous gates to the Braithwaite Estate slowly swung open as the taxi arrived, then the winding journey up the approach to a huge mansion on the hill in the distance, lit brightly from the inside.

"I need you to wait," said Phipps, as they pulled up to the mansion.

"It's the end of my shift," said the driver.

Phipps passed the driver a few credits, they both nodded.

The front door to the mansion opened before Phipps had a chance to ring the bell.

"You're late," said the woman standing in front of him in a maid's outfit, the type you would see staff wearing in mansions such as these.

Phipps nodded. From behind the door, she pulled out a large spade, and handed it to him, then a flashlight, then an old sock and finally, a dog's lead with a brown Labrador, Brandy, at the other end. Phipps checked his notes, reached in his pockets for the doggy treats, fed the dog a few, and then rubbed the sock about Brandy's nose. In a flash she was off, escaping Phipps' grip on the lead, and into the darkness. Phipps followed in hot pursuit, as he fumbled to turn on the flashlight.

13
PRISON RIOT

By previous arrangement some of the inmates in another of the Green River prisons were asked, and had agreed, to create a diversion. They didn't know what for, but they were up for it. The prison in question was Green River 8, a dangerous place filled with rapists, murderers and all manner of other dangerous criminals. The entire prison was run on the inside by Wolf Backman, more dangerous than most and Jack had thought long and hard before asking him to arrange a diversion, he decided he had no choice, but he would now be in Wolf's debt and that made him uncomfortable. In the west wing of Green River 8, the inmates were stirring. It was midnight, and they were beginning to make a racket with everything at their disposal. Warden Walter P Courage observed the activity from the desk in his office on the 13th floor. His monitors were switched to Green River 8 only and he jumped through the cells and other rooms in rotation. Finally, he flicked the communications switch on for Green River 8,

"Gas in five minutes, this is not a drill," he barked, as red lights

above Green River 8 illuminated.

"Gas, Gas, Gas," yelled the inmates as they made even more noise. Guards in the facility scurried back to their respective quarters to fetch masks in preparation.

****

In the sports hall of Green River 5, all was quiet, until the clock struck midnight.

"Go, go, go," shouted the professor.

With that Jack hit the start button and all hell broke loose. In an instant the metal knuckles sprang into life and with them, the giant opalescent wings, the noise, a deep penetrating hum, the like of which had never been heard before. The giant mirror bowed and flexed and the spider web holding it to the walls stretched to near breaking. The craft veered left and one of the wings brushed the sports hall wall, making yet more noise, like that of a playing card, attached to the spokes of a kid's bike, only faster and louder, much louder. Jack struggled until he finally had the craft under control, and at that moment, the mirror broke its tethers, and at precisely 12:03am, came crashing down on the sports hall floor.

At midnight in the canteen Millie was speaking to Danny, she had her script, she knew what to say, then suddenly a huge deep droning noise filled their ears.

"What the hell is that?" said Danny springing to his feet.

"Danny," said Millie, but he was already running towards his quarters.

"Wait," she said as she gave chase.

Danny ran to his desk, Millie in hot pursuit, caught the door just in time, and followed him in. Danny made for the monitor at his desk and flicked through the cameras, everything looked ok. As he settled on the sports hall, he was distracted by a message that popped up on his screen…Gas, Green River 8, 12:05, this is not a drill. Danny repeated the words aloud.

"That must be it," said Millie helpfully. Danny span around, surprised,

"You're not supposed to be in here Millie, you have to leave".

Over his shoulder, on the monitor, Millie saw the mirror fall, and as it did, the craft behind it, airborne and out of control.

"I mean it Millie, I'll lose my job," said Danny, and with that Millie kissed him. He moved his head to one side, and she kissed him harder.

Back in the sports hall the engines had been cut and focus turned to getting the gigantic mirror back in position. Bob Gosling had his leg crushed in the accident, and they were later to find that it had been broken in three places. Two of the group helped Bob back to his cell before re-joining the others in their mammoth effort. Yellow lights began to flash around Green River 5, standard procedure when another facility was going to gas.

"You'll have to go Millie," said Danny as he finally broke from their embrace. *"I've got things to do, procedures to follow,"* he said

as yellow lights flashed about them.

Millie tried to kiss him once more, but Danny was resolute, he shuffled past her and headed for the door as Millie once more focused on the chaos in the sports hall on the monitor.

"Now Millie," he said, as he grabbed a gas mask, *"You can't stay here".* "

Why the mask?" said Millie,

"It's procedure," he said, *"Green River 8 is going to gas, and I need to do the rounds and you need to get back to your cell".*

Millie was panicking, perhaps she should have gone further, she thought, already through the canteen, and well on the way to the cells. Help came from a very unlikely place, in the form of Bob Gosling, leaning up against the wall outside his cell, leg covered in blood.

"Jeez Gosling, what the hell happened to you," said Danny,

"I fell," said Gosling.

"Some fall, we'll need to get you to the infirmary, Millie back to your cell, can you walk Bob?"

"I'll try,"

and with that Danny put his shoulder under Bob's arm and they headed slowly to the infirmary.

Warden Walter P Courage sat at his desk, excited, he loved to use the gas. This was his fifth gassing, by contrast Phipps and Williams had never gassed. But Courage knew the rules back to front, and this was most certainly an infringement of section 247 of the United States Federal Penal Code. The red lights had been flashing in Green River 8 for four minutes and at the stroke of 12:04am the sirens began to sound. A red light shone above the dome of Green River 8, in his office on the 13th, and yellow lights above the others. He flicked the comms on,

"one minute to gas," and in the prison,

"gas, gas gas," shouted the inmates, louder than ever.

He loved it, and he waited in anticipation, excitement mounting until, finally he flicked the switch. Over to the dome to watch the gas emitting from the little pipe, then back to the monitors to watch the inmates slowly fall asleep collapsing where they stood. Finally, when it was all over, he leant right back on the swivel chair at his desk, arms folded behind his head, a big grin on his big fat face, he loved this job.

****

At 12:05am, Phipps wandered, in near darkness, through the woods of the Braithwaite estate, looking for Brandy. He could hear her, moving closer to the scratching with every step, until finally, there she was pawing at the earth, in front of him. He breathed a sigh of relief, took the treats from his pocket, and offered them to his partner in crime. Brandy sat beside the hole she had started, chewing away as Phipps began to dig. After what seemed an eternity to Phipps, and at the bottom of quite a shallow hole, the spade made the noise of metal hitting metal, and he knew at once he had found the chattel. Falling to his knees, with the flashlight in his teeth, he worked the soil around the parcel with his hands. It was well wrapped in plastic and sealed with tape.

"Jeez, this is heavy" he mumbled, as he freed it from the earth and lifted it onto his lap.

Brandy circled him excitedly and he gave her more treats.

"Well done Jack, we make a great team," he said breathlessly, and in no time at all he was on his way back to the city and Hanks Printer Repair.

****

Work continued to fit the mirror back into place in the sports hall and finally, using all the spider web they had, and some makeshift pulleys that had been built earlier to lift the wings into place on the craft, it was back where it needed to be. The professor checked the angles using the basketball court lines, some minor adjustments and the job was done. The crew filed out of the sports hall, exhausted but happy, their mission complete, leaving Jack and the professor behind. The two men looked at each other in silence for a moment before embracing and laughing.

"Did you think she'd fly Freddie?" said Jack,

"Oh yes," said the professor, *"I knew she'd fly, but what I don't know yet is how the hell we're going to fly her out of here!"* They both laughed.

"Can you imagine if that mirror were made of glass, we'd be scuppered then for sure," said Jack

"If it were glass, and even if it didn't smash into a million pieces, we'd never have been able to lift it," said the professor.

More laughter followed and at that point the sports room door opened, it was Danny Maguire, and he didn't look happy.

"What the hell are you two doing in here," he said angrily, *"There's been a yellow alert for the last few minutes, and you should be in your cells with the others, you know the drill".*

At that point, the yellow alarm lights stopped, in the sports hall, the prison, and all the other prisons in that office on the 13th, and the two men made their way towards Danny and the door, and then on to their cells. On the way back Danny told them of Gosling's fall on the way down from the sports hall, both looked as shocked as they could. Jack thought of Millie, he now wouldn't see her until the following morning 8:00am, he hoped she was ok.

****

Phipps pulled up outside Hanks Printer Repair at 3:00am, paid the driver some more credits, and carried The Bayze, still wrapped in plastic to the shop door. The place was in darkness, Phipps looked for a bell but couldn't find one and eventually pulled at the door, it was open.

"You're late," came a voice from the shadows, *"It's 3:00am".*

"You said you were always here," said Phipps sarcastically, as he placed his heavy parcel on the counter.

"Come with me," said the man, lifting the countertop, as Phipps followed him to the back of the shop.

"So, you must be Hank?" enquired Phipps.

"Do I look like a Hank?" said the man, *"no, you can call me Raj, the last owner was Hank, I bought the place from him when I was 16"*

Impressive thought Phipps, an industrious young man, he liked that.

There on Raj's worktop were three identical cases, and if you had offered Phipps a million dollars, he would not have been able to tell which one he brought in a few hours earlier. These three cases were identical, even down to the scuffs and scrapes, the scars of use.

"Ok," said Raj, *"This one's yours,"* as he took the middle of the three and set it behind him on the floor. *"This, the outer and this, the inner,"* he said as he pointed at each of the two remaining cases.

He set the first case on its side, span it around, flicked the locks and opened it, to reveal what looked like the contents Phipps had removed as instructed before he left his apartment earlier.

"Wow," said Phipps, *"That looks just like…"*,

"Yup," said Raj interrupting, *"That's the false top, I'm quite pleased with how it's turned out, considering the photos you left me,"* as he lifted it on hinges to reveal a completely empty case below.

"Wow," said Phipps again. *"How did you manage that?",*

"3D printer did the work on all of this, those pencils will wiggle around a bit and the first few pages on the notepad, but it is a false top, so best not to touch it," he said, as Phipps was about to.

"This is the outer," he said as he opened the other case, *"It fits exactly into this one,"* as he lifted the first case into the second and snapped the locks shut.

"Hey presto," he said as he handed Phipps one case with another identical one within it. *"Amazing,"* said Phipps. He was genuinely impressed.

"Now throw it," said Raj.

Phipps followed instructions and threw the case about three feet in front of him. As it hit the floor, the inner case jumped from the outer case, and both snapped shut.

"Hey presto, then there were two!" said Raj, as he walked over and picked up the two cases, put one inside the other as before, and handed them to Phipps as one case.

"They are extremely strong and very light but be careful when you set them down as the spring for the separation mechanism is very sensitive".

"What about my case?" asked Phipps.

"We'll get that back to you". Back to me thought Phipps, that wasn't in the instructions.

"Oh, one more thing," said Raj, as he handed Phipps what looked like a retro transistor radio. *"You can open that with a clip on the side,"* he said pointing, *"I don't know what that's for, they never tell me anything, but it's probably for that parcel you brought in".*

Phipps gathered up the cases, the radio, the parcel, and left, he was never going to get a cab in this neighbourhood at this hour, he thought.

TIME FLY

14
AFTER THE STORM

Jack stared at the ceiling of his cell, excited by the success of the test flight, but worried about Millie and wondering how Phipps was getting along on the outside. All members of the crew on the east wing, apart from Jack, Millie and Elspeth wondered why there was such urgency for the test flight, it felt much more real than the drills they had done previously, had Jack really worked out a way to fly them to freedom? There were only 6 seats on the aircraft and 12 of them, would they be one of the 6 left behind? Elspeth stared at the ceiling also, reminiscing about her life before jail on The Braithwaite Estate, walking the grounds with Brandy, she missed the life she had. Millie sat awake, wondering about Phipps, thinking of the chaos of the sports hall she saw on the monitor. Did they rescue the situation? She had no way of telling until the morning. Then there was the kiss with Danny, not the worst kiss she'd ever had. That night the crew, laying in their cells were mostly awake for one reason or another, by contrast, every inmate on Green River

8 slept soundly.

****

Phipps had walked for over an hour to get home, the cases, and their contents, very heavy indeed. He entered his apartment just before 5:00am utterly exhausted. He slumped in his chair, with the picture of Lucy clasped firmly to his chest. He needed to be up in 3 hours and the thought of what lay ahead worried him greatly. He fell into a fitful sleep where he sat, waking just before 8:00am.

****

The crew made their way to the canteen, as they always did at this time, but today was different, there was a palpable sense of excitement in the air, as Jack slid in beside Millie on the bench.

"Morning," he said,

"Morning," she replied,

"and?" he asked,

"and what?" she said.

"And, well you know, and?" said Jack stumbling over his words.

"First base," said Millie.

Jack sighed,

"Good," he said, *"that's good,"*

"Couldn't even get to second, you lot were making far too much noise," they both laughed.

"How did you get on, I saw the chaos on Maguires monitor?"

"Everything is back as it should be, the mirror undamaged but Gosling is in the infirmary",

"I know," said Millie. *"He has three breaks in his leg, Maguire told me last night on his way back, couldn't happen to a nicer guy,"* she paused. *"Mind you, if it weren't for him, you would have been rumbled."*

"Let's hope our luck holds out," said Jack.

Elspeth joined them, *"Well, he made it there and he has the item,"*

"Yessssss," hissed Jack, leaning towards the breakfast table, clenching his fist.

"How do you know?" asked Millie.

"I had the maid send a message to me about a fictious relative dying if the mission were successful, it came in on the comms this morning".

Danny Maguire walked past the table and without stopping said

"Palmer, you are on report for not being in your cell on yellow alert last night and Mrs Braithwaite, I was sorry to read about your niece,"

Elspeth looked up at Danny and smiled, and they all shared a giggle as Danny Maguire marched off.

"Is it time to tell the others?" asked Elspeth.

"*Not yet,*" said Jack, "*I might tell Freddie later but let's wait for the Warden.*"

15
SMUGGLER

Warden Phipps decided to skip breakfast, he had so much to do before leaving. He kicked off his muddy shoes, deciding to clean them that evening, and headed for the shower. He fitted The Bayze snug inside the transistor radio casing, and the radio, inside both cases and headed for the office. This case is really heavy, he thought many times on the journey, but particularly as he climbed the subway stairs. As he had expected, all went smoothly through each of the security checks, with the last before the lift, three guards, three desks, and a better than average chance of a favourable result.

"Please not number three." Phipps whispered, again and again under his breath.

"Number three today, Phipps," said the guard sitting at desk three.

No, no, no, thought Phipps, as beads of sweat began to form on his top lip, he paused for a moment, before moving slowly towards the desk, surely the game was up. He set his flask down on the desk, and quite by accident, whilst trying to heft the heavy case, knocked the guard's coffee over, leaving a puddle all over the guard's workspace, he swung the case back down by his side.

"Jeez Phipps, you need to be more careful, go to number two",

"I'm really sorry," said Phipps.

He turned around and headed for desk two, setting the case down, flipping the catches, opening it and spinning it around to be examined by guard two. Phipps couldn't watch, he turned around again, went back to desk three to pick up his flask and waited. He didn't see guard two wiggling the pencils, or thumbing the notepad, he just stood and waited for what seemed like an eternity.

"OK," said the guard.

Phipps turned around retrieved his case and in no time, he was heading to the 13th in the lift. That was a genuine accident he thought, someone up there was looking out for him, maybe, just maybe, this was meant to be. He arrived at his office breathless, his shirt soaked in sweat.

"Morning Phipps," said Warden Walter P Courage, as he entered, *"You missed a show last night, gassing on 8, oh, and a casualty on 5, the reports are on your desk, all pretty straightforward, I've cued the playbacks on 8, and I am sure you'll countersign my report as this was a clear infringement of section 247 of the federal penal code. I've brought up the relevant section on the screen, they need your sign off by noon".*

"Ok said Phipps," as Warden Courage left for the day.

Phipps slumped in the office chair, halfway there he thought, as he set about the task of reviewing the night's activities; the chat with Palmer would have to wait.

Jack was getting jittery, it was 11:30am, and Phipps was supposed to have called for him at 10:00am sharp, something must have gone wrong. He went to the yard and looked out of the dome to the misty shapes beyond. Jack could see that someone was sitting at the desk, but he had no way of telling who. For months the inmates had observed these shapes to the extent that they knew the shift changes, two large shapes rather than one, and they knew the Wardens' names, but that was it. Jack went back inside to join the others, it would only be a matter of time before they were questioned, after all, who would have use for an illegal time machine? The inmates on the east wing of Green River 5, that's who, the game was surely up.

"Palmer to the communications room, five minutes".

Jack breathed a big sigh of relief, thoughts raced through his mind, there had been a problem, Phipps had a change of heart, couldn't get The Bayze in, any number of permutations. One thing was certain, that was definitely Phipps' voice, he was there, and he had asked to speak to Jack. In no time at all, Jack was in the comms room staring at a camera, waiting for Phipps to speak.

"It's here," said Phipps finally.

"That's great," said Jack. *"How did you get on?"*

"I was up most of the night, the journey to Connecticut was straight forward though, I got the cab to wait and bring me back".

"Cab," said Jack nervously, *"I thought you were taking your own car?".*

"It was downtown, I normally get the subway, and I was running very late" said Phipps. *"Is there a problem?"*

"No" said Jack quickly, but he was lying.

If they were able to change the past, the cab driver would have a residual memory scar of his trip to Connecticut, it would not have been a routine ride, what would he have done with the fare, what would he have bought with the money? This added a layer of complexity to an already difficult mission. By contrast, those affected by Lucy's tragic and untimely death, would have a deep residual memory scar, like a nightmare but, their new reality would be one they would wish to accept as true, and provided they did not share their nightmare with others affected, all should be well. Jack calculated that each of the adults touched by Lucy's death, the funeral, the loss, would not readily discuss this horrific nightmare, who would? And the children, well they would be least affected, if at all by these time tremors. Kids were tough in their innocence, dealing with new things everyday of their lives, until the inevitable onset of routine, as they got older. Everyone in on the ruse would also feel the tremors, but they were prepared and if they pieced it all together it wouldn't matter anyway.

"I was worried about you," said Jack, *"We were supposed to speak a couple of hours ago"*

"I've been doing reports all morning, a gassing in one of the other facilities, which reminds me, what happened to Gosling?" said Phipps.

Jack paused for a moment,

"he had a nasty fall on the stairs down from the sports hall, a broken leg and a bruised ego",

"Good," said Phipps. *"I'll file that now, so what's next?".*

Jack went through the new list of instructions before leaving the comms room. Phipps pondered his own departure from the 13th floor later that day with great trepidation.

Jack headed straight to the sports hall to speak to the professor about the newly acquired Bayze.

"Wow Jack, I'm amazed, you are a clever fellow," said the professor.

"Not as clever as you Freddie, you are the cleverest person I know," said Jack,

"This is true," said the professor, *"I'm the cleverest person I know."* He smiled and continued, *"There was one other man, during the second world war, Alan Turin, a mathematician, who broke the Enigma code and shortened the war by…"*

"Focus," snapped Jack, *"Are we ready?",*

"As ready as we will ever be," said the professor with a big grin.

"Good," said Jack, *"Both Mille and Elspeth know everything but please don't tell the others, not yet",* the professor nodded.

Danny got up from researching at his desk and went straight to see Millie.

"Hi Millie, I looked in on Gosling earlier, his tibia is broken in two places and a further break to his fibula, they were transverse compound fractures, unusual for a fall, I'm sure they'll give him Tylenol for the pain, and with the help of an external fixation device, he'll be up and around in no time."

Millie smiled, *"Thanks for letting me know Danny, oh and I'm sorry about coming into your room, thanks for not putting me on report."*

Danny's face went crimson, and he scurried off without a word.

****

It was time, Phipps gathered up his flask and case as Warden Williams arrived,

"8 Bells, Josh?" asked Harry,

"8 Bells," said Phipps.

"Hey Josh, Stella said she'll do ribs next Thursday, how does that sound?"

"Perfect," said Phipps, his mind very much elsewhere, as he headed for the door, and along the hallway with the shagpile carpet to the shrink portal.

Just before 6:00pm, Phipps pressed the intercom and as always, it crackled into life,

"Go ahead."

"Warden Joshua Phipps, shift number 17,215 complete, permission to leave the facility?"

"Please hold," said the box.

And at that very moment Phipps took one step forward, threw himself to the floor, and his case through the portal. It instantly disappeared, as he knew it would, as the machine powered down.

"I've tripped," he shouted at the box, *"damn shagpile,"* he added.

"Hold on," crackled the box, *"We're sending someone up".*

Phipps had no time to waste, now on his hands and knees, he scampered across the shagpile and onto the white marble beyond the silent portal, pressed his cheek to the cold floor, where were those damn cases? Nothing, a vast expanse of nothing, he looked ahead of him, the exit lift, was leaving the ground floor, no time to waste, he pulled his spectacles a little from his nose, and rolled them around, to amplify his view, there in front of him, two tiny dots, the separation mechanism had worked perfectly in miniature. He crawled closer circling the dots, without taking his eye off them for a second, now on all fours with his back to the lift. At once, the lift doors opened and Phipps heard the voice of Randy Herber behind him,

"We were not expecting this Mr Bond," he quipped, as he came up behind Phipps.

"Lost your case?" he said as he bent down looking at the marble, hands rested on his knees,

"There she is," he said as he licked his finger and pressed it on one of the tiny dots,

"This will have to go into security, you ok, Mr Bond?" he said as he examined his finger closely.

"Yeah, I'm ok," said Phipps as he licked his finger and pressed it on the remaining case.

This was not part of the plan; Phipps was supposed to retrieve both cases, hand them over at Smallz, one to be returned later partially grown, which he would take back to security claiming it had stuck to his shoe. He had no idea if the case at the end of his finger was the right one. He prayed his luck would hold out.

16
SMALLZ

Smallz was no ordinary caterers, more a laboratory than a kitchen and considering the number of customers the company served, it was quite small. In the food prep area, staff in white lab coats busied themselves about the place, looking into huge microscopes and taking notes on clipboards. At the beginning of the operation there were many spools with what looked like various colours of cotton wrapped around them, these microscopic meals, were being sliced at one centimetre intervals and dropped onto a conveyor belt, to be sliced more finely when they reached their destination. Periodically a pea would pop from a machine in the wall and roll onto the belt. At the end of the production line there was a huge magnifying glass to observe the various dishes as they passed through and at the end, any number of tiny tin trays into which the food was dropped. This was a state-of-the-art food processing plant, serving up endless meals in miniature. Herb sat on the first floor of the building in his office which had a large glass window to the lab below, so he could keep an eye on things.

There was a knock at the door,

"Yes," said Herb loudly, a young man entered,

"You know you were expecting that delivery, well there's a guy here, I think it's him, but he won't hand anything over, and he's insisting on seeing the boss, and that's you."

Herb sighed, something's not right, he thought.

"OK bring him up."

Within a matter of minutes, the door opened again, and Phipps entered.

"Yes sir," said Herb, *"Please take a seat, what can we do for you?"*

"I was asked to deliver a small package here at exactly this time," said Phipps as he sat down,

"And what does that have to do with me?" said Herb,

"Well, there's a problem," said Phipps.

Herb weighed up his options; on the one hand he wasn't sure if he could trust this stranger, and on the other, if there was a problem, he needed to know about it.

"Well, I'm not sure I can help you sir but why don't you explain your problem, and we'll see what we can do."

Phipps fumbled in his pocket, pulled a postage stamp out and handed it to Herb. On the back of the stamp was a tiny square dot, stuck to the glue,

"That's the problem."

Herb took the stamp, pulled a huge magnifying glass from his desk drawer, and examined the dot.

"Ah," he said finally, *"Lost luggage from the Palomino resort, someone's going to be mighty relieved when they get this back."*

Herbs eyes levelled on Phipps, and Phipps eyes levelled on his, like two gunfighters ready to draw, neither had any idea what the other one knew.

"Yes," said Phipps, thinking for a moment and then, in a matter of fact sort of way, *"It might be empty,"*

"Hmmm," said Herb, *"Not our problem, we'll get a description logged and get it back to its rightful owner,"* all the time holding Phipps stare, *"Well thank you Mr?".*

"Thank you," said Phipps without giving his name as he got up to leave, finally breaking his stare. Within minutes Herb took the stamp to the shop floor.

****

At 8:00pm that evening, right on time, the kitchens of Green River 5 received their daily delivery and importantly, a package on The P Train. Some years earlier, those running the penal system in the US had decided it would be a good idea to remind prisoners of their miniature predicament, as it was easy to lose that perspective inside. So, apart from the cleverly designed domes which, to the inmates, showed ghostly shadows of enormous Wardens pacing around outside, a pea was delivered to each of the prison kitchens every week. Prisoners were given washing up duties on rotation, so at least twice year, would cast their eyes on a giant pea, reminding them of just how small they were.

"It's here," said Elspeth, just back from the kitchens as she held out a transistor radio, in front of the Professor.

"Jeez, we've done it," said the professor, *"Well, Jack's done it,"* he said correcting himself.

"We've all done our bit Freddie," said Elspeth reassuringly, *"Not least you, you built an aircraft."*

The professor smiled as they headed off together to the sports hall. Behind the mirror they met with Jack and Millie, and they watched as the professor opened the transistor radio casing to reveal The Bayze. Within a few minutes they were inside the aircraft, The Bayze was dropped into the hole that had been provided for it, a fat fibre optic cable was attached to the top of the machine and more cables were plugged in. Two digital dials flicked into life in the cockpit.

"Everything looks ok," said the professor, *"When do we go?"*

"One hour," said Jack, as the others looked on in amazement.

"An hour?" said the professor.

"Why not," said Jack, *"No time like the present, the four of us will meet back here, and we don't tell the others, not yet."*

Elspeth, Millie and the professor looked at each other, as Jack tapped the dials in the cockpit, they knew they must trust him, he'd not steered them wrong yet.

By the time Phipps got back to his apartment, he was

exhausted. He had been on the go now for pretty much two days solid and he had not slept properly for weeks. He slumped in his chair, the picture of Lucy pushed to his chest, and just after 9:00pm, fell into a deep, deep, sleep.

17
ICE CREAM

The four travellers met one hour later behind the mirror in the sports hall. They all huddled around a makeshift drawing Jack had prepared of their destination earlier.

"Ok," said Jack, *"Here is the ice cream parlour, across the road from the park, weather conditions that day were good, sunny with very slight westerly winds, so we'll arrive here,"* he said, pointing at the road between the park and the parlour.

"What about traffic?" said Elspeth,

"We'll jump 30ft above the road," the professor chipped in,

"It's too risky to start the engines here, so we'll start them when we arrive." "There will be a drop initially," said Jack, *"But once they kick in, we can pull up and take a good look at the event."*

"So, it's time?" said the professor,

"It's time," said Jack and with that, they all clambered inside

the craft.

Millie and Jack sat up front in the cockpit, Elspeth and the professor in two of the four remaining seats behind them. Millie and Jack went through the pre-flight checks flicking switches as they went, the dials in front of them became illuminated with a reddish glow. Jack rolled the dials for longitude and latitude, Millie checked and rechecked the coordinates.

"That's a roger go on cords,"

then to the time and date, as Jack rolled the dials, again Millie checked,

"That's a roger go on time," Jack turned to Millie,

"Are we a go for the jump?",

Millie made one last pass on the dials

"We are a go for jump, repeat a go for jump,"

Jack looked behind him, at the other two passengers,

"Hold on tight," he said before depressing the dial.

A light filled the fibre optic cable above The Baze, the passengers' faces bathed in its blueish hue and then all at once, THAWOOOOO; the inside of the sports hall behind the mirror was empty.

The craft arrived right on time, right where it should be, and began a long fall. Red lights flashed immediately on the cockpit dash as an alarm bell sounded. Jack hit the start button for the engines, they fired into life, still falling as Jack wrestled with the controls, falling further, until finally the craft came under control, Jack looked at Millie and smiled. Millie wasn't smiling, over his shoulder through the golden bulbous window on his side of the cockpit, she saw a large arctic lorry approaching them fast.

"Up," she screamed as loud as she could,

Jack looked at her confused, in a split second, Millie unstrapped herself, lurched towards Jack and pulled back the joystick as far as she could. They cleared the front of the lorry, but the slipstream sent the craft downwards, three legs hit the top of the lorry, sending them skywards again, and finally it was gone. Everyone breathed a sigh of relief as Millie brought the craft back under control.

"Thank you Millie" said Jack *"that was quick thinking, Freddie damage report,"*

The professor looked around him,

"All looks ok to me, I'll look at the undercarriage later, but those carbon fibre legs are up to the job" .

They positioned themselves over the place where the accident was to happen and began to film with the four cameras that sat on the underside of the craft. The whole incident from Phipps leaving Lucy, crossing the road to the parlour, and then the crash took less than three minutes. After the accident they continued rolling until the professor thought they had seen enough.

"OK, it's a wrap," he said, *"Jack, find somewhere to land, we'll power down and jump back."*

With that Jack flew to a quiet corner to land and within an instant, THAWOOOOO, they were back where they started in the sports hall, less than 10 minutes after they had left.

For the next couple of hours, the four travellers watched and rewatched the accident from every single angle and discussed strategies for changing the past. It was tiring work, watching a child lose their life again and again, until finally a break through. Elspeth sat bolt upright in her chair.

"We're looking at this all wrong, no offence guys, but we are focusing on changing the direction of the car, and too many things could go bad. Even if we could get inside the driver's side window and distract the driver, the car is already out of control as it makes the turn, and we would be inside a car that was certain to crash. Look at Lucy, she's looking from the park, I think she sees the warden coming out of the shop with the ice creams, and look, she takes three steps forwards, just on the edge of the park and the pavement. What if she didn't see the warden leave the shop?"

The four travellers set about making a plan, which they hoped would work and with preparations complete they were ready to jump again.

"One last thing," said Elspeth as they walked towards the craft. *"Surely, if we are successful here and Lucy didn't die, does it then not naturally follow that Phipps didn't help us to help him, he didn't go to my place, and he didn't dig up the Bayze in the first place, as we've changed that right?".*

"No" said the Professor, *"You are quite wrong, The Bayze is here, it is now in our possession, and it was a necessary part of the plot to change the past. It is an inanimate object, if you were to go back to the*

estate, the Bayze would not be there, as it is here." He continued, *"If you look at Einstein's theory of…"*

"Hold on, honey" said Elspeth interrupting, *"So long as we get to keep the toy, that's all I need to know."* They all laughed.

About three weeks earlier, Phipps was in the park with his granddaughter Lucy. He did this every week, and every week he looked forward to it, and every week they both had fun. Phipps watched as Lucy played on the swings, then the merry go round, and then back to the swings. She was having a fine time, as she always did.

"Fancy an ice cream?" shouted Phipps from the bench he was sitting on,

"Yes please Gramps," said Lucy as she played with the other children.

"Stay right here, I'll be back in a jiffy," and with that, Phipps waited for the traffic, and after a huge artic lorry and some other cars passed, he crossed the road to the parlour.

As he opened the door to walk in, he didn't notice the fly above his head.

"I'll take two Mr Softies please Mam", he said as he approached the counter, *"Lots of sprinkles and chocolate sauce"*,

"Yes sir", said the assistant, *"Coming right up," "That'll be eight credits,"* and with that Phipps set the money on the counter.

The assistant handed him the cones, one in each hand and he headed for the door. Just at that moment, a fly landed right on his nose, Phipps waved his arm in front of his face, the fly flew off, only to land directly back on his nose. Phipps waved again, and the fly was off, this time right in front of his eyes, another wave and one of the scoops came clean out of its cone and hit the floor.

"Jeez," said Phipps as he headed back to the counter, behind him a terrible screech, and the sound of a car crashing outside the shop on the opposite side of the road.

"Lucy," he cried as he ran from the shop dropping his ice creams, across the road to find Lucy standing behind the mangled wreck, screaming, a body slumped on the car bonnet, blood everywhere.

"Thank goodness, little one," he said as he scooped her up in his arms and moved away from the steaming wreck.

That was too close, he thought, it could have been very different.

18
HANK'S PRINTER REPAIR

Herb picked up the phone on his desk and tapped at the buttons,

"Hanks Printer Repair," said the voice at the other end of the line, *"We've got a problem."*

Sometime later, a man dressed in a delivery uniform, wearing a turban, walked into a nondescript building somewhere in New York and headed past many uniformed guards to the main reception desk.

"I'm here to pick up a briefcase for a Mr Phipps," said Raj.

"You'll need to go to the security window," said the guard, waving over his shoulder.

Raj headed to a small window behind reception to another guard,

"I'm here to pick up a briefcase for a Mr Phipps," he said once

more.

"Ha," said the guard, *"The case of the shrunken case, you got a letter of authority?"*,

"No," said Raj, *"But I can describe it for you, apparently he can't get into his apartment as the keys were inside."*

The guard thought for a moment and then he walked to the back of the room and picked up two cases, holding them in front of him,

"That one," said the man pointing.

The guard brought the case back and set it on the counter in front of them, he tried to open it, it was locked.

"Well, it's back to full size, you can take it, but you'll have to sign."

The man in the turban squiggled on some paper and he was gone into the night.

A little later that same man, this time dressed top to toe in black, still wearing a turban, fiddled with the locks outside Warden Phipps apartment, within seconds he was in, down the hallway, past the kitchen, he could see the back of Phipps head, sitting in a chair, snoring. On the side table in the lounge, just behind where Phipps slept, was a pile of books, pencils, pens, and some paperclips. The man set the original case down beside them, pulled a photograph from his pocket and began to place the items, one by one, and in a very particular way. Phipps stirred once or twice whilst he was there but, very soon he was done, he padded silently down the hallway to the front door, pulling it quietly behind him, and he was away, into the night.

19
A NEW DAY

Phipps woke up in the chair at 8:00am. He felt different, he was cheerful, he couldn't remember falling asleep in the chair and he couldn't remember why he might not have been cheerful previously. He kicked off his shoes and headed for the shower, he was looking forward to breakfast at the deli.

"Good morning, Mary," said Phipps smiling as he arrived,

"Morning Josh, usual for Josh Bert, you look happy?"

"Yeah, it's a beautiful day," he said as he slipped into the booth. *"Hey Mary, I'm not sure if I mentioned to you at the time, but Lucy nearly got hit by a car at the park a couple of weeks back, a joyrider, came up on the sidewalk, missed her by inches, he was just a kid, killed instantly. Today I'm counting my blessings for everything that's good in my life and Lucy is the best, she's over this evening for a sleepover".*

Mary stared to the floor,

"You didn't mention Josh, I don't think so, but a lucky escape for Lucy, she is the best."

Mary remembered a dream, in the way that one does when one hears or sees something that reminds them. She couldn't remember when, but it was more a nightmare than a dream, she resolved to keep her mouth shut, and wandered back towards the counter.

****

Elspeth had the professor cornered in the canteen,

"Listen honey," she began, *"You know I'm the only one in this joint who hadn't jumped before yesterday."*

The professor nodded,

"And I'm the one that knows the least about how all this works,"

the professor nodded again.

"So just answer this, yes or no, and none of your fancy physics, if I were to travel back in time to where I was before, would I see me?".

"Yes" said the professor.

"But how could I be in two places at the same time, there's only one of me?" asked Elspeth.

"There is only one of you at any one time," said the professor,

Elspeth looked puzzled.

"You are not in two places at the same time, you are in fact in one place at different times".

"Ok, ok," said Elspeth.

"Same time tomorrow?" said the professor smiling,

"Same time tomorrow", said Elspeth, as she got up to leave.

****

Millie was looking for Jack, he wasn't in the yard, the canteen, the games room, nor was he in his cell. Millie headed to the sports hall, that was the last place to look, he must be there. But as she rounded the mirror, she saw nothing, no Jack, and no craft.

"Jeez," said Millie to herself, *"He's jumped on his own".*

Millie didn't know what to do, what if he didn't come back, where had he gone, and why had he gone? So many questions. At that moment THAWOOOOO, and the craft appeared in front of her eyes, in just the same place as it always was, only this time it was covered in a film of dirt, and what appeared to be a large rock embedded in one of the wings. Millie clambered aboard the structure, opened the door, and there in front of her, sat in the cockpit, was Jack.

"Where the hell have you been Jack?" she said, *"You should see the state of the outside of this thing, the wings broken for sure."*

Jack turned around to face her, a large gash on his forehead,

"Test flight," he said unconvincingly, *"I wanted to test her in extreme conditions",*

"Extreme conditions," said Millie angrily. *"She won't fly again until*

that wing has been fixed, if she flies again, you are lucky to be back here at all, what were you thinking Jack?"

Jack looked at the floor of the cockpit and without looking up said,

"It was him, it was Jimmy."

Jack reached for a switch on the cockpit dashboard, the monitor came to life, and Millie watched the flight recording.

****

Phipps whistled as he walked to work, it was a sunny day and after his shift he was seeing Lucy again, unusual for a weekday but, his daughter was at some function or other, and Lucy was having a sleepover. Up he travelled to the 13th floor and into his office,

"8 bells Harry," he chirped,

"8 bells Josh," said Harry.

"Hey Harry, I'm looking forward to those ribs, Thursday, wasn't it?",

"It can be," said Harry puzzled. *"I'll need to check with Stella, but we're not on rotation, so why not!"*

Harry looked at Phipps, but Phipps was preoccupied with some paperwork on the desk,

"I'll let you know," said Harry as he left.

Phipps flicked the communication switch to the east wing of Green River 5.

"Palmer to the communications room, five minutes," he said.

He paused to think, and for the life of him he didn't know why he needed to speak to Palmer, he must be getting old he thought, he rechecked the reports, it would come back to him, ah Bob Gosling, that was it.

****

Jack and Millie heard the announcement from the cockpit of the craft,

"I better go," said Jack,

"This is not over," said Millie, *"And don't ask me not to tell the others, I'll have to tell Freddie and Elspeth and I'll tell the rest that the sports hall is out of bounds for now, and what do you think Phipps wants, do you think he remembers?"*

"Let's hope it's a small residual memory scar, these early days are the most important, if all goes well, we'll have a new normal in a day or two," said Jack as he left for the communications room.

Phipps watched as Jack arrived to take the seat.

"How are you doing down there?" said Phipps,

"I'd rather be elsewhere," replied Palmer.

"So, Palmer, how's Gosling doing, he got out of the infirmary this morning."

"I've not spoken to him yet, but I will do so later today," said Jack. *"I can get back to you tomorrow with a report".*

Jack thought it a good idea to speak to Phipps again so he

could monitor the progress of his new reality, as far as that was possible.

"And what happened to your head?" said Phipps, *"I banged it on the TV monitor in the games room, its nothing,"*

"It doesn't look like nothing to me, get someone to look at it," said Phipps, *"And come back to me tomorrow once you've spoken to Gosling, that will be all".*

****

After Millie had finished reviewing the flight recording, she made her way to see Elspeth and the professor. She told them everything.

"I'm not happy," said the professor, *"This is most irregular, Jack should really have known better,"*

"Hold on," chipped in Elspeth. *"It's obvious he has his reasons,"*

"I understand the reasons," said the professor. *"What I don't understand is why he didn't tell us, not even Millie, he has put everything at risk here, and we, as his friends, should have been told, I'm sure we could have helped."*

They all agreed on that and the three of them waited for Jack to return.

"The four of us are going to the exercise yard Jack, we need to talk, and you need to know, I'm not in the least bit happy," said the professor as Jack entered the canteen.

"So, you've told them", said Jack to Millie.

"Yes she has," said the professor, *"Too many secrets here, and if*

*we are to get through this, we need, you need, to make some solemn
promises going forward. If this was the second world war, there would
be a court martial for sure,"*

Jack hadn't seen this side of Freddie, he didn't like it, and he
began to realise how foolish he had been, in not sharing vital
information with them all earlier.

"Come on honey," said Elspeth, *"We will get through this, but let's
start by going back to the beginning, and you…"* she paused, *"You,
will tell us absolutely everything."*

Jack nodded and he started to tell the tale of that fateful day,
many years ago, when he was just a kid, as they all walked
together to the exercise yard.

****

Phipps was having a good day, it was an easy shift at work,
and he had ribs to look forward to on Thursday. Or at least
he thought so, Harry had been weird in not remembering
the invite. He also had Lucy tonight for a sleep over, he
must get those shoes cleaned. Warden Walter P Courage
entered the office for the shift change.

"Evening Warden Phipps, anything to report?"

"Not really," said Phipps, *"8 is very quiet today, gas hangovers I
guess, 3 still has problems with the drainage, but they will take a look
at that tomorrow, and one out of the infirmary on 8, and one in for a
check-up, the reports are on the desk".*

"Did you sign off on the gas for 8?", said Courage,

"Yup, all done," said Phipps as he left to go home.

Down the shagpile to the shrink portal, you could trip on this he thought.

****

The four travellers walked and talked in the exercise yard.

"What I don't understand is how you ended up outside the house in the dust storm?" said Elspeth.

"It was me," said Jack, *"I was positioned by the door to the yard outside, observing everything below me, and I came in, well 'young me' came in from the yard, and as the door was pulled open, the craft was sucked out and all hell broke loose, a loud bang from above, I lost power and hit the jump button."*

"Yes, but this is all academic," said the professor, *"There's no way you can go back to try to change this outcome Jack, this was nearly 30 years ago, the time tremors would be earthquakes, it's just not possible, you do know that don't you Jack?!"*

"Yeah, I know that," said Jack, *"But I just needed to see what really happened, I had my suspicions, but I needed to see for myself."*

"And motive?" said the professor,

"I don't know, I got there just as Jimmy pulled the trigger,"

"You mean your brother James?" said Millie.

"Yeah," said Jack, *"The whole family called him Jimmy."*

"Ok," said the professor, *"It's settled, we'll jump back, I'm coming with you this time,"* he said looking in Jacks direction. *"And earlier too, we'll watch the whole thing unfold, and we plan meticulously before we jump. Agreed?"* They all nodded. *"Millie how bad is the*

damage?".

"I'll take a proper look at the fuselage, but the wing is shot for sure, and we'll need help from the others to fix that, I think we should get it cleaned up, and then tell the others that the wing was damaged during the test flight a few days back, that's one thing I still agree with Jack about, we don't tell them, not yet." They all nodded.

"We'll do this once Jack, and that's it, agreed?" said the professor.

"Agreed," said Jack.

"One last thing," said Elspeth, *"I vote its Jack's job to break down that boulder,"* they all laughed.

****

Phipps arrived at his apartment that evening, still in the best of moods, he checked the time, I'll get those shoes cleaned, he thought. He went to the wardrobe; the shoes were filthy. Where did that mud come from, he pondered, oh well, and back to the kitchen. Lucy was due any moment, he picked up the picture, it felt strange, the sort of feeling you have when you've just remembered you had forgotten to do something important. His thoughts interrupted as the doorbell rang

"Lucy Lou," he said as he opened the door,

"Gramps!" exclaimed Lucy, *"Thanks,"* said his daughter, *"I'll pick her up from school tomorrow. Be good for Gramps,"*

"I will," said Lucy.

This was Lucy's first sleepover and Phipps was delighted.

He went to the kitchen, got some chocolate, put a kid's animation on, habitually he picked up the picture again and slumped in his chair,

"Want to watch with me?"

"Yeah Gramps," sang Lucy as she bounced onto his lap.

He held her close, he felt strange, something was off, he resolved to put these feelings to the back of his mind for now, he would enjoy Lucy's sleepover.

20
BACK TO SCHOOL

"Next lesson?" said Elspeth,

"Sure," said the professor, as they sat in the canteen.

"I understand that The Bayze is not there, because it is here, but is there still a hole in the ground where The Bayze once was?"

"Oh yes," said the professor, *"Just as there is a radio casing for the Dayze, and those clever uses, they were all part of the now reality we live in, a reality with Lucy now back with us."*

"Hmmm," said Elspeth, *"The bit I don't understand is why didn't all those things just disappear, as they were only created in order for us to change things, before they even existed?"* The professor smiled,

"Yes, but they were all necessary to make things as they are now, so therefore it follows that they must, by definition, be in our new reality, the one we created by changing the past."

"Jeez," said Elspeth, *"You really are twisting my noodle now."* The

professor smiled again,

"You are asking the wrong questions, the real dilemma here is in the perceptions of the people affected by the changes we have made. We have changed the past, if nobody were around, nobody would have noticed, you could have gone back and dug 100 holes in the woods, and that would not affect anybody because, nobody would have noticed. The past is all about people's perception of it, sometimes their own memories, sometimes shared, and often different from one perspective or another, but always their perception. Jack and I are betting on the single idea that even if, all those affected by the loss of Lucy's life in their old reality remembered it, their desire would be so strong to believe their new reality that they would push anything else from their minds." He continued, *"It's very early on, the next few days are crucial to the success of the mission, if we are not exposed in a day or two, we have succeeded, and who knows what will become of Lucy as she grows up, that has not as yet been written in what will become, in time, her own life story".*

21
LESSONS FROM THE PAST

The four travellers set about getting the craft back into shape, three cleaning up the fuselage and Jack, charged with breaking down the boulder, which, on the outside, would have been a tiny speck of dust. He had the hardest job as penance for his earlier jump.

"How are we going to get rid of all this?" said Jack pointing at the big pile of detritus after he had finished.

"Simple," said the professor, *"We will do as the prisoners did, in the Second World War, in Stalag Luft III."*

"Pray tell," said Elspeth.

"Well, in the camp the huts were built too far from the perimeter making an escape by tunnel near impossible. One British officer inspired by the story of the Trojan horse, came up with a plan to start a tunnel, using a vaulting horse as cover. Each morning, the vaulting horse would be put in the same place, and a prisoner was carried out

in the horse, and each day he dug. The earth he dug up was hung on the inside of the vaulting horse in bags and the following day, the prisoners spread the earth in the yard".

"But how did they do it without the guards seeing?" said Elspeth.

"Well, quite ingenious really," said the professor, *"They had holes in their pockets tied with string, they filled their pockets, went to the yard, pulled the string, and the earth would fall down their trouser legs."*

"Is that even true?" said Millie,

"Quite true," said the professor.

Modifications were made to their prisoners' uniforms, and for the rest of the day they made trips out to the yard periodically to get rid of the dust.

With the help of the others, the wing was repaired, and they were ready to jump again.

They had planned meticulously. Jack and the professor had rewatched the flight recording over and over, and calculations had been made to ensure they arrived at exactly the right spot to watch the event from the right perspective. This time it was just Jack and the professor, Millie was to stay behind to distract Danny if necessary, and Elspeth was to keep watch over the sports hall to ensure none of the others went behind the mirror whilst the craft was gone. Jack rolled the dials for longitude and latitude, and this time it was the professors turn to check and recheck the coordinates.

"That's a roger go on cords," he said as he then turned to the

time and date. *"And that's a roger go on time,"* Jack turned the professor. *"Are we a go for the jump Freddie?"* *"We are a go for jump, repeat a go for the jump".*

THAWOOOOO! In the blink of an eye, the inside of the sports hall behind the mirror was empty again. The craft was in freefall, lights flashing and alarms sounding in the cockpit, but for the briefest of moments, Jack was getting used to this manoeuvre, he immediately righted his ship, and climbed to the ceiling near the corner of the room. The professor hit the video and they observed the room below them. Jack saw his mother in the kitchen looking out of the window smiling, she was looking at him. Jack's father picked up his hat from the table, hugged Jimmy, kissed his wife and made for the door. Jimmy moved to the cabinet drawer where Jack knew the revolver was kept, pulled it out and pointed it at his mother. She turned, saw Jimmy, and moved towards him. Jack could see his father moving off in the car outside through a second camera, and then bang, Jimmy shot his mother in the head. She dropped to the floor lifeless, and blood began to cover the kitchen floor.

"I'm so sorry Jack," said the professor, *"I think we've seen enough, it's time to jump back."*

Jack was frozen, it was no easier seeing this for a second time.

"Jack," said the professor again, *"Jack, it's time, we have to go,"*

and with that Jack snapped out of his trance, landed the craft, shut down the engines and hit the jump switch, THAWOOOOO. They were gone.

Back in the sports hall, Jack and the professor sat in the cockpit in silence for what seemed like an eternity. The professor resolved not to move until Jack was ready, and then finally he spoke.

"I thought there would be a reason..." whispered Jack, *"that we would see something, anything, to make sense of this all."*

"It was a very sad affair," said the professor, *"I can't imagine how it must make you feel."*

Jack fell into silence once more, it had changed him, he was a different Jack now.

22
LIFERS

The time travel inmates on the east wing of Green River 5 had a reasonably easy life compared to the other wings and prisons, they could pretty much come and go as they pleased; even their cells weren't locked at night, although they were supposed to be in them at certain times. Everything on each wing was controlled by the 'live-in' guards, and the east wing had just one, Danny. Green River 8 by contrast was all lifers, not death row, they were in another office on the 13th floor, but these guys were never getting out. There were no professors here to design aircrafts and no time machines, if this lot were going to see the light of day, they had to do it in a more conventional way. The boss of Green River 8 was Wolf Backman, nobody was sure if Wolf was his real name, but nobody was going to ask. Wolf began to run things after he had squared up to the previous boss, and they had agreed to have a good old-fashioned dust up in the canteen the following morning. Wolf made sure he had the edge; he got hold of some of the paint used for the prison walls which was impervious to the cell shrink beams and painted himself from top to toe. By the time he came out of his cell the next morning he was at least twice the size of his opponent, and he beat him half to death. The other guy ended up in a wheelchair and was transferred to another facility. Wolf got three months solitary, but his place at the top of Green River 8 secured. He had managed to get plans of the Green River 8 facility with details of everything, and they were making plans of their own.

****

"I'm really worried about Jack," said Millie, *"He just isn't himself,"*

"Who would be," said the professor, and they all agreed.

"We need to find out more about Jacks brother, I mean what kid kills their mother, never mind motive," said Millie as her brow furrowed and she hung her head in despair.

"I'll open up a conversation and see where it goes," said Elspeth softly as she slowly got up and wandered over to him.

She approached calmly, *"Hi Jack,"* she was met with silence.

His gaze didn't alter, it remained on the floor, but she could see his body was more rigid and his eyes welling.

"Aww honey, how are you doing?" said Elspeth sympathetically.

"Well, I've just watched my kid brother kill my mother in cold blood," he paused and took a breath, *"Twice!"*

"Just awful," she replied, *"what was he like?"*

Jack went on to explain that they were twins, and Jack was the eldest by six minutes, there had been problems with Jimmy's birth, he didn't know what, but his parents had always joked about Jimmy's reluctance to come into the big wide world. Elspeth listened patiently. Jack and Jimmy, without any other family, went into the system, firstly together, but a couple of years in, they were separated, there had been problems with Jimmy, but again Jack didn't know the detail. Elspeth made a mental note of the name of the children's home, and anything else Jack said that she thought might be relevant. Jack and Jimmy had stayed in touch for a few years, but communications were broken off when Jack was about 13 years old.

Elspeth was very resourceful, in the way that especially wealthy people are, without money as a barrier, she could get her hands on pretty much anything, as pretty much anything can be obtained, at the right price.

****

Wolf and his close circle looked over the blueprints for the Green River 8 facility. The plans were very detailed, as blueprints are, including a floorplan of the prison, the size of the plate on which it sat, the dimensions of the glass dome and, even the table and its height from the floor, although no mention of the floor covering on the 13th. The table sat higher than normal, rather like one you might find in a bar to stand around. It stood 3ft 6 inches high, with a glass dome on a plate on the top. The dome went right to the edge of the table, and at its base was a rubber seal to ensure the dome was airtight, save the pipe that pumped in the fresh air. The inmates decided, since the air pipe was too high to reach from their perspective, the rubber seal was to be their exit. Prisoners, since prisons were invented, had devised ever more ingenious plans to escape their captors, they had time, time to think things through to the very last detail, and the inmates in Green River 8 had more time than most. The 3ft 6inch height from the tabletop to the floor presented the first problem as, for the tiny prisoners, this represented a sheer drop of over 2,000ft. A long thin bucket was designed which would carry three prisoners from top to bottom, and two journeys would be made from the dome to the floor. A 3D printer would be needed to make the bucket in miniature, - which full size would have been the equivalent of 3ft across and 4ft deep. All they now needed to do, was work out how they were going to break through the rubber seal.

****

Elspeth and Millie sat in a huddle discussing Elspeth's earlier conversation with Jack.

"Awful," said Millie when she had finished.

"I'll arrange to get copies of the files from St. Annes Children's Shelter, I've a friend in the judiciary who can help with that, you see what you can research in the news around that time. Jack was there for five years, but Jimmy left after about two, and this is between us for now," said Elspeth.

Millie nodded and headed straight to see Danny, he would unwittingly help her in her search, she thought.

"Hey Danny," said Millie, as she met him in the corridor between the cells and the games room.

"Hello Millie, how are you doing?"

"I'm well, thanks. I've been thinking about a friend of mine who has been back in touch recently, I was in the army with her. She was brought up in care."

"Who's that Millie?" asked Danny,

"Oh, she's called Jackie, I can't imagine what it must be like to be brought up as a child in that way, I always had my parents, and those schools are a mixed bag, I think hers was ok from what she told me, it was St. Annes Children's Shelter in Illinois".

Danny made a mental note of the school's name,

"I better get on Millie, I've got the rounds to do, I'll see you later,"

"See you Danny," said Millie as they parted company.

After Danny had finished his rounds, he sat at his desk, researching the US care system in general and St. Annes Children's Shelter specifically.

Bob Gosling sat in the games room, watching TV, his leg, rested on another chair, stretched out in front of him, in a plastic boot. Jack sat next to him,

"How's the leg?"

"I'm on the mend, three breaks, but they reckon this thing can come off in a month or so and I'll be as right as rain."

"Good," said Jack.

"How did the test flight go?" asked Bob,

"Yeah it flies, there was some damage to the wing but it's all fixed now",

"So we just need a plan to fly us out of here?" enquired Bob.

"Yeah," said Jack quietly whilst he looked at his shoes, *"All in good time,"*

"All in good time," repeated Bob *"We've got plenty of that, right!"*

Jack smiled. He would request a meeting with Phipps right away. Jack made his way to see Danny,

"Hello Mr Maguire,"

"Hello Palmer, what can I do for you?"

"I've been asked to report to Warden Phipps,"

"And the nature of this report?"

"He asked me to go back to him on Gosling today,"

"Ok, he'll call for you." As Jack left, Danny turned and under his breath, muttered to himself, *"Think's he runs this joint."*

23
SECOND THOUGHTS

Phipps, still in a good mood, arrived at the office at the usual time. He had enjoyed the sleepover with Lucy, she had been safely delivered to school, and all in all his world was good.

"8 Bells Harry?"

"8 bells Josh, Palmer had his check-up in five, just a bruise, but he has a request to speak with you. The guys are coming in at 11:00am to check the pipes on 3, Oh, and Stella can do Thursday for ribs, she's wiggled things around, we'll see you at 8:00pm."

"Marvellous," said Phipps.

Wiggled things around he thought?

"Palmer to the communications room, five minutes," said Phipps after Williams had left.

Jack was soon there waiting for Phipps to speak; he would try to read the situation which was difficult when you couldn't see who you were talking to. Phipps watched Palmer, this was all a bit pointless, he thought, why had he asked to see Palmer about Gosling, he had the medical report on his desk, but there was something, some reason, he couldn't remember, but the feeling was not a good one.

"How are you doing down there?" said Phipps finally,

"I'd rather be elsewhere," replied Palmer.

"So, how's Gosling getting on?"

"He's fine, I saw him this morning in the games room,"

"Ok, that will be all,"

"Oh," said Jack in surprise, *"Ok,"* and he left.

All appeared to be going well, he thought.

Phipps sat in his office chair, thinking of Palmer, a previous meeting, the picture of Lucy then in his mind, pain, terrible pain, a taxi, three briefcases. He put his hands in his jacket pockets and pulled a piece of plastic out, a sweet wrapper, he thought. He examined it, it was orange and white, with a single word still visible, 'doggy'. The blood drained from Phipps' head; he had remembered, at least he thought he had.

****

Later that day, Danny bumped into Millie again, well he deliberately bumped into Millie again.

"You were right about the care system being a mixed bag in the US," said Danny, *"There's some real horror stories, but St. Annes is one*

of the good ones apparently,"

Danny refrained from telling Millie that he had checked and there was no Jackie ever registered at St. Annes. He didn't want her to think he was being nosey, and anyway she could have gone by a different name them, he thought.

"Since the incident, and that was about 30 years ago, long before your friend would have been there, everything has been fine, in fact it's won awards," he said.

"Incident?" said Millie,

"Yeah, there was a couple that ran the place, the man shot his wife in cold blood, they'd had a big argument, and he shot her, two in the morning. Thank god the kids were asleep, he denied it, of course he would, he did up until his death a few years back."

"Tell me more," said Millie.

"Not much to tell really, it was his gun, his prints all over it, powder on his hand, one of the staff came down and saw him standing over her body with the gun, open and shut really."

"Aw," said Millie, *"I don't know what I would do without you in this place,"*

Danny went crimson once more and scuttled off.

Millie found Elspeth in the games room, it was busy, so she caught her eye, nodded and Elspeth followed her back to the cells in the women's dorm. Millie recounted the conversation with Danny a few minutes earlier, leaving nothing out.

"*Good girl Millie,*" said Elspeth, "*The reports won't be here until tomorrow, and we'll take a look through them, my contact is going to follow Jimmy through the care system, where he went after St Annes, we'll see what we can find and take it from there.*"

"*Good,*" said Millie, "*And Jack?*"

"*No,*" said Elspeth, "*Lets collect as much information as we can, I'll brief the professor, but I think we should only speak to Jack when we know more, he's a bit shaky right now, and who can blame him.*"

"*Ok,*" said Millie,

"*Apparently the meeting with Phipps was brief but seemed to go well, everything is on track.*"

"*And the incident at. St Annes?*" said Millie,

"*Oh, I think we should take a look, don't you?*" said Elspeth,

"*Hell yeah,*" said Millie, and they both giggled.

Elspeth briefed the Professor as planned.

"*So, you want to jump with Millie?*" "*Yup,*" said Elspeth. "*Millie can fly, I'll set the coordinates, but we can't let her go alone.*"

"*Why don't I go instead of you?*" begged the Professor.

"*No, you need to stay, and keep Jack busy, you know how he is now, and we need a safe pair of hands here whilst we are gone, someone who can manage him, someone he respects.*"

"*Ok, but we are going to go through the drill until you know it in your sleep,*" instructed the Professor finally, "*When do you want to jump?*"

112

"As soon as possible,"

"Ok," said the professor, *"we better get started."*

24
NEEDLES

Green River 8, like lots of other prisons in the system, had a drug problem, and it was quite common for partners, on conjugal visits, to smuggle in hypodermic needles. These were kept small by being continually exposed to the ever present shrink beams. Every now and again, a needle would be kept from the beams, to be later used as a shank once it had grown to a useful size, and these weapons were deadly. The Guards tried to keep on top of the situation, but these were needles after all and could be easily hidden in plain sight. Wolf was being visited by Sandy, his long-term girlfriend. She was in his biker gang on the outside, their chapter was The Five Roses, out of San Diego, on the Mexico border, with Tijuana over the wall. The gang ran drugs across the border; Sandy was born to smuggle.

"Jeez Wolf, who are you killing this time?" said Sandy, as she passed him the needle, *"That thing's big enough to put a horse to sleep."*

She was right, Wolf had asked her to get the biggest needle she could find, and what she handed him was the type used by vets to sedate large animals.

"Never you mind Sandy girl, now you get over here and gimmie some of that sugar," he said as he pinned the needle into the lining of his prison uniform and pulled her towards him.

25
A NEW DISCOVERY

The professor and Elspeth were sitting in the cockpit of the craft going over the jump protocols again and again.

"Ok, let's try another scenario," said the professor, *"You are going to 1944, just at the start of the Battle of the Bulge,"*

"Jeez, honey" said Elspeth, *"Does every scenario have to be during The Second World War?"*

"It's as good a place as any to practice using these dials, if you get one single digit wrong, you could end up in completely the wrong place or completely the wrong time, or both, and as you know, that could be fatal, and never mind you two, where would we all be then, stuck in here, that's where!"

"Ok, I get it, 1944, give me the rest of the date and the time?"

This went on for a long time until the professor was satisfied that Elspeth understood the importance and could move the dials at a reasonable speed. Millie joined them,

"How's our student?"

"She is doing well, I think we are done."

"Did you know," started Elspeth, *"The Battle of The Bulge was a German offensive to prevent allied forces from taking the port of Antwerp."*

"Who won?" asked Millie,

"We did," said Elspeth, *"No offence Freddie,"* they both smiled.

"Ok," said Millie, *"There's no time like the present, let's go now, Freddie, you'll keep Jack busy until we get back. Elspeth thinks the reports regarding Jimmy will arrive tomorrow, so we'll see what that turns up before we speak to Jack, agreed?"*

The professor nodded and left Millie and Elspeth in the cockpit preparing for the jump whilst he went to find Jack.

****

Phipps sat behind his desk in the office, his face ashen as he wrote down what he had remembered. There were fragments of a conversation with Palmer, he remembered a trip in a taxicab, he remembered three cases, digging something up, a dog, he didn't even own a dog, but most of all he remembered Lucy, the tragedy and then, the near tragedy. What was he to do, he knew he had done something wrong, he knew Palmer had helped him, and he knew he was involved in changing the past.

****

"That's a roger go on the co-ords, and that's a roger go on time

honey," THAWOOOO, and they were gone.

Elspeth and Millie found themselves in the kitchen, in the basement of St. Annes Children's Shelter, then the fall, lights and alarms until Millie fired up the engines, left then right as she wrestled to get the craft under control until finally it was level and they climbed close to the ceiling in the corner of the room.

"This is good," said Elspeth, as they rested in place, the flight recorder already on.

They saw a woman at a kitchen sink washing dishes, there were two sets of stairs, one in each corner and they had eyes on both. A man came down the stairs that were situated behind her, she turned around, he was waving his hands and pointing at her.

"They look like they are arguing," said Millie.

In the craft, video was always in black and white and audio muffled, coming in and out like voices on the wind. The professor had explained earlier that this was something to do with interference from the Lanthaneodinium in the Bayze, but naturally, his explanation was much longer! The woman also waved her hands about and pointed to the door, the man turned around and walked back up the stairs from which he had appeared earlier. The woman turned back to the dishes.

"Look," said Elspeth.

She pointed over to the shadows in the corner of the room where they saw a small child climb to their feet, moving slowly to a side table behind the woman. From one of the drawers, the child pulled a gun, moved a few steps closer to the woman, but as she turned there was a bang, and she dropped to the floor. The child dropped the gun beside her, moved slowly back from where they came, and again crouched in the shadows. The man was seen running back down the stairs over to the woman, bent down beside her, then as he stood, picked up the gun, at the same time another man came dashing down the same set of stairs. He froze for a moment, then approached the first man attempting to take the gun from his hand, they began to fight and fell to the floor. The child rose from the shadows again, the men still wrestling on the floor, jumped over the lifeless body of the woman, and was gone up the second set of stairs.

"We've seen enough," said Millie.

"Hold on," said Elspeth as the two men, still rolling on the floor, were joined by a third, and then another.

The three men disarmed the first man, but not before another shot was fired into the ceiling. Two held him down whilst the third went to a telephone on the wall and made a call.

"Ok," said Millie, *"I'm going to land over there, we'll cut engines and jump back."*

THAWOOOO, they were back in the sports hall, Elspeth turned to Millie, and Millie to Elspeth, they both looked at each other in disbelief.

****

Phipps sat at his desk trying to piece everything together and the only thing he thought he could be certain of was the two versions of what happened that day at the park a few weeks earlier. In one version Lucy was tragically mown down on the edge of the park and the pavement and, in the other, a near miss; he knew which version he preferred. But what was he to do? He knew, or at least he thought he knew, he had been a part of the plan to change that outcome. Who else had been involved? It must have been Palmer, that much he was quite sure of, but others, there he drew a blank. His thoughts were interrupted by two workmen who had come to have a look at the pipes in Green River 3.

"You're late," he said not looking up from his desk,

"Sorry boss, traffic is a nightmare this morning, which one is it, they all look the same?"

"You'll find the numbers etched on the glass of each one, 3 is over there," he pointed.

"Ok thanks," replied one of the workmen as they both moved to the right dome.

"How long do you think this will take?" asked Phipps,

"Hard to say until we've had a look, can I get the logs from when the problems began?" asked one of the workmen.

Phipps obliged and after some reading, the workman said, *"We'll have to swap it out,"*

"What the whole prison?" said Phipps.

"Yup there are blockages all over the place, best to change

the whole unit, it's an easy job."

Easy, thought Phipps, easy for you, you just need to pick up one tiny prison and replace it with another, it's us who will have to ensure all prisoners and their belongings are out before you do. Phipps had prepped for this once before and it was not easy.

"Ok, let's get it scheduled and we will do the necessary this end," said Phipps.

"Ok," said the man, *"Sign here,"* as he handed Phipps a clipboard.

"Keep away from the other domes," said Phipps to the second workman, who was hovering around Green River 8, the man stepped away.

****

The next day, Elspeth and Millie awaited the reports about Jimmy Palmer with some trepidation while the professor was briefed on what they had seen in the basement kitchen of St. Annes Children's Shelter. He too was shocked, and they all agreed that they would not say a word to Jack until they knew more. After looking through the reports Elspeth went to find Millie.

"So there were five other care homes, but by the time he was 18, the trail goes cold," said Elspeth,

"Well we've plenty to be getting on with for now," said Millie.

"This might be a bit much for me to be talking to Danny about though,"

"Already ahead of you honey," said Elspeth, *"My contact is going to look for any news items related to each of these homes around the times that Jimmy was there, apparently it shouldn't be too hard as he was at each for just a year or two years at most."*

"And Jimmy's report from St. Annes?" said Millie.

"Well, all we know," started Elspeth, *"The shooting was written about with regards to the welfare of the children, and that Jimmy was the only one not moved by the incident".*

"Jack has never mentioned it, so however he felt at the time, he doesn't seem to remember it now." Said Millie

"The report mentions that Jimmy was an unemotional child, but beyond that it's not specific, it feels to me like each of these homes were handing on a problem without acknowledging what that problem actually was." Elspeth concluded

26
THE TUNNEL

Wolf and his crew were in the exercise yard of Green River 8 watching a basketball match. To the side of the court was a sort of makeshift seating area, to allow inmates to sit together to watch the game. The area had four tiers of bench seating and each bench could seat up to 10 inmates, the top tier rested a foot or so away from the glass dome. Wolf and his closest crew were the only ones allowed to use these seats; there was a hierarchy, where you sat, indicated how important you were in the gang. Meetings would take place, agreements would be made, and basketball would be watched on these benches. When the benches were even partially occupied by the inmates, the view behind them would be obscured from the cameras, and it was here that two inmates were working away at the rubber seal at the base of the dome. The plan was a simple one, the hypodermic needle that Sandy had smuggled in for Wolf had been hidden from the relentless shrink beams and had now started to grow. It was about the width of a broomstick, it had been cut to about one third its size, one end sharpened like a razor, in the other end a black rubber stopper had been plugged. The inmates forced the large needle right into the rubber until it was flush with the inner surface of the seal, the rubber plug in the needle and the colour of the seal were a perfect match. A large piece of wood was jammed between the back of the benches and the rubber seal over where the needle had been pushed in, to ensure the needle would not grow into the glass dome. Now all they had to do was wait, as the needle grew, it would push steadily outwards, and at full size, a tunnel to the outside world.

****

Phipps made the necessary arrangements for a swap out of the main Green River 3 building, so a replacement could be fitted the following day. The workman was right, the job was an easy one for them, they had a spare part at their workshops, and all Phipps needed to do was ensure preparations were made for 2,000 or so prisoners, guards and other staff to be out before the swap was made. The new facility was to be an exact replica of the last, so once everyone was evacuated from the building, the premise a fire drill, prisoners would be gassed, the dome lifted, and the entire facility replaced. Prisoners would wake up and everything would be exactly the same as it was before they fell asleep. But for Phipps there was much to do, procedures to follow, everything needed to be orchestrated so that when Warden Courage was in to oversee the swap, everything was in order, he was a stickler. Phipps was happy to have the distraction of the swap out to take his mind off piecing together the events that had taken place over the preceding days, although try as he might to put it completely from his mind, it kept invading his thoughts. He resolved to have a good think that evening back at the apartment and then decide what he was to do.

****

Wolf had chosen five of those closest to him to make the escape, two of the inmates were also members of the 5 roses chapter and it was the three of them that would go first. The bucket had also now been smuggled in, together with a roll of the finest silk thread, and this was to be their makeshift lift down the sheer drop to what waited below. Both the bucket and the thread had been left behind the benches at the side of the basketball court to grow back to their normal size, away from the shrink rays. It was a risk that these items would be discovered, but Wolf was betting on the fact that the guards would not pay too much attention to the exercise yard whilst it was empty, and the benches provided excellent cover. The plan was to make good their escape at the next exercise session the following day assuming the bucket and thread had not been discovered, and the brace between the bench and the end of the hypodermic needle had held. If the other end of the needle were sharp enough, then it would have pierced the outer of the rubber seal and there would be a perfect escape tunnel 1.6mm wide to the outside world and, freedom. Wolf didn't sleep much that night, he stared at the ceiling wondering if the plan would work, dreaming of a life outside with Sandy and the gang, he could almost smell the fresh air, the freedom. He didn't have long to wait now, he thought.

****

The following morning Warden Courage had been put on rotation to oversee the swap out on Green River 3. Well, he had requested it, he had done one before and he was delighted that in no time at all he would be carrying out another gassing. He went over Phipps' paperwork from the preceding day, checked and double checked everything until he was satisfied all was in order. Two workmen arrived and were asked to wait outside in the hall until Warden Courage was ready for them. He joined them both in the hallway. He recognised one man, Billy Hawthorne, the other younger man, a new guy.

"Mr Hawthorne," he began, *"I'm looking for a Standard Inmate Facility, part number PFS20510, do you have the right part?"*

"Yes sir," said Billy, as he showed him his paperwork.

"Ok, let's see it," said Courage.

Billy carefully took the part from a tool kit, *"Here it is",*

"Ok, that looks about right. I've a few more things to go over, I'll call you in when I'm ready, there's a coffee machine down the hall, shouldn't be too long now," and with that Courage went back into his office and closed the door.

Behind his desk, he flicked a comms switch,

"Warden Walter P Courage, we are ready for the part swap,"

"Roger that Warden Courage, please hold," said a faceless voice. *"We are prepped and ready for the seal release in T minus 30 minutes,"*

"Roger that control," said Courage, *"Evacuation in five,"*

"Roger that, evacuation in five," control replied.

Warden Courage checked the time, made a note in the log and waited. Precisely five minutes later, he flicked the comms switch to Green River 3,

"Fire, fire, fire, please evacuate the building this is not a drill, repeat this is not a drill."

Red lights began to flash, and alarms began to sound inside the dome and inside the prison walls of Green River 3.

In the misty distance beyond their dome, Wolf could see a faint red haze coming and going, it was time he thought.

"Hey Bull," he said, *"It's happening, we've got 15 minutes,"*

"We're ready boss," replied Bull as the inmates queued to go out of the door to the exercise yard.

Wolf and his crew made their way directly to the benches, others joined them there on the basketball court.

"This is going to be one hell of a game," said Bull as they took their seats.

Two of the crew went behind the benches obscured by the crowd. Shortly afterwards, Wolf felt two tugs on his prison uniform trousers from one of the guys behind the benches. Two tugs meant the thread was there along with the bucket, and one had been attached to the other. Wolf waited, another two tugs, this meant the rubber cap at the end of the needle had been removed and that the needle had made its way to the other side. Wolf breathed a sigh of relief, had the needle not made it through there would be no means of escape and all their efforts would have been in vain. Wolf waited again for what seemed like an eternity for the next signal as the basketball game began in earnest, to the cheers of the crowd.

Warden Courage sat behind his desk, waiting to hear from the head guard in Green River 3. The comms crackled into life,

"The cells are cleared and locked down Warden Courage, we are doing a sweep of the building now, and we're locking up as we go,"

"Roger that, very good, keep me posted," said Courage as he looked at his watch, all was going to plan.

Courage got up from his desk, put his head around the door,

"Five minutes," he said to the workmen sitting outside,

"Ok boss," said Hawthorne.

Courage went back to his desk, all his monitors focused on Green River 3, he looked through each cell block making notes in the log as he went. All cells were clear, so onto the other rooms in the building one by one,

"Let's count down those rooms,"

"Roger that," said the guard as they both went through the long list of other rooms in the facility.

One by one, Courage flicked the monitors and double checked.

"All clear, repeat all clear," said the voice,

"All clear," repeated Courage, another switch, *"This is Warden Walter P Courage to Control, we are all clear here and requesting permission to gas,"*

"Please hold," said the voice, and then,

"That's a roger for gas, we are releasing the seal in T minus 10 minutes."

Courage got up from his desk, put his head around the door,

"You better come in now," he said to the workmen.

He didn't notice the younger man's tattoo of five roses on his forearm as he rolled up his sleeves ready to put the new facility in place, nor did he notice the positioning of the open toolbox right below the dome of Green River 8 which was situated right next to the Green River 3 facility.

"It's time," said Wolf to Bull,

as he nodded at a third man, they all got up from their seats and stood in a huddle by the side of the benches.

"You ready?" he asked.

The two others nodded as more men joined the group and Wolf and two other men moved behind the benches hidden by the assembled crowd. Wolf looked down the inside of the needle, he could see nothing beyond, but he knew they had made it through, a gentle breeze moved from the dome out of the aperture, blowing his hair. It reminded him of riding his Harley in the open air, it felt good, and freedom was close, now the long journey down. The makeshift bucket lift was placed into the aperture of the needle and the three men climbed in at an angle whilst another four held the silk rope which was wrapped around the bench to act as a pully. Once in, the four men began to let the bucket move slowly down the inside of the needle and beyond, faster now as the bucket descended to ground level. Wolf looked over the edge and saw the shape of a blue box below, the underside of the table above them, and the singular table leg beside them as they went down, the blue shape getting slighter larger as they travelled downwards. The pace quickened as they fell but it still seemed to be taking forever, this might be just 3ft 6inches, but from their perspective over 2,000ft or just over a third of a mile.

Warden Courage flicked the comms,

"The fire has been isolated, repeat the fire has been isolated, please hold there, you'll be back inside in no time,"

prisoners cheered unaware that this was code for the guards to don their masks in preparation. Warden Courage flicked another switch to kickstart the gas. He loved this bit, he jumped up from his desk and moved over to peer inside the dome as the gas took a grip and the inmates began to drop one by one. He watched transfixed for a good two minutes before dragging himself away, a few more checks at his desk before,

"How are you going down there?"

"Yup all good here, gassing successful." Another switch was flicked,

"Warden Courage to Control, gassing complete, we are ready for the seal to be released,"

"Roger that, please hold." He waited for a few seconds, and then, *"Ok seal is released you are clear to swap, repeat clear to swap."*

"Ok guys," said Courage, *"Over to you, and for heaven's sake be careful."*

The two workmen positioned themselves at either side of the dome and lifted it together away from the plate and onto a workbench they had put at the side.

"Ok let's get the old one out," said Hawthorne to his workmate as they both positioned themselves once more in readiness.

The lift went smoothly, and the old facility was placed on the workbench next to the dome. *"Ok let's have the new part,"* said Hawthorne.

His workmate reached down inside the blue toolbox. The workman was crouched right next to the table leg of Green River 8 and directly in line with his eyes he saw the tiny bucket descending to the toolbox below, they would be down shortly, he thought, but he'd need to buy some time if others were to escape.

Wolf, Bull and Razor descended further in the bucket, moving very fast now. At the top the men were mostly letting gravity do the hard work until a mark in the silk thread was approaching, to signal to them that the bucket was nearing the bottom. Calculations had been made to measure the exact distance from the floor to a tray inside the toolbox where they were to land, no account had been made about the shagpile carpet as they weren't aware of that, and the bucket hit the tray in the toolbox with a thump. The three men scrambled from the bucket across the blue floor and to a box no larger than a quarter the size of a standard match box, they clambered in, the box lined in cotton wool.

"Strap in," said Wolf, as he tied makeshift threads around his legs, waist, and chest under his arms, *"It's going to be a bumpy ride,"*

they watched upwards and saw the bucket disappear into the distance. At the top more men joined the effort to pull the bucket back up to the dome, this was not easy as they had the weight of 2,000 feet of silk to drag up from the depths, so progress was slow.

Warden Courage watched as the new part, now retrieved from the toolbox, was ready to be set in place,

"Does that look bent to you?" said the workman pointing to the side of the facility,

"Give it me," said Hawthorne,

"We don't have time for this gentlemen," said Courage.

"Nonsense," said Hawthorne, *"I don't see anything, these parts are as precise as they come. It was made by 3D printers, and I've not seen a wonky wall in 20 years, now let's get this finished".*

The workman retrieved another piece of equipment from the toolbox, as he watched the bucket slowly travelling upwards, it looked rather like an industrial desk lamp with an LED screen at its base and a grasping arm at the other end. Hawthorne pressed a couple of buttons, and the tool sprang into life, picking up the new part in one sweep and moving it to hover over the plate.

"All set," he said,

another button was pushed, and the entire building began to lower slowly towards the plate as Courage watched on intently.

Within moments the facility was in place, a green light shone at the base of the crane contraption, and it moved away to a resting position.

"All done," said Hawthorne, *"You'll just need to get an inside check from your guys on the ground."*

Courage moved back to his desk,

"Can you give me an alignment check please?"

"We are on it," said the voice, *"It's a fit."*

"Ok," said Courage, *"You can get the lid back on,"*

referring to the glass dome and the two men positioned themselves, as they had before at either side of the plate and carefully reset the dome in place.

The prisoners behind the benches had managed to get the bucket back up to the top, but they had underestimated the sheer weight of the silk thread at full stretch, and they were running well behind schedule. Three more inmates got into the bucket and this time the descent was going to need to be a fast one.

"Thank you gentlemen," said Courage, *"Good job, reseal on 3 please Control,"*

"Reseal complete," came the voice, and as the workman bent

down to put the old part and the arm back in the toolbox he saw the tiny bucket, this time much higher, they were never going to make it. He couldn't delay things long enough without jeopardising what had already been achieved, they were on their own now. He closed the lid of the toolbox and picked it up very gently and they headed for the door. Courage bid them farewell and went back to his desk oblivious to the fact that six inmates had escaped the dome of Green River 8 and that three of them were currently making their way out of the building.

The second bucket load continued to descend until the mark on the silk appeared at the other end of the thread, the descent slowed and then halted. The bucket swayed just six inches above the shagpile carpet,

"I'm going to jump," said one of the three, as the bucket began to rise again very slowly,

"Don't be an idiot," exclaimed another, *"You'll never survive the fall, that's got to be a 300ft drop!"*

"I'm not going back there," he said defiantly, as he climbed from the bucket and jumped to the floor below.

The bucket stopped rising and began to descend again. Word had got to those working behind the benches that two of the three misty shapes had left the office and their escape vehicle with them, they decided to give the passengers more rope so they could at least reach the bottom, they also resolved to try to do the journey as many times as they could before yard break was over. The two remaining passengers eventually got to ground level and what they saw was not what they had expected. The prisoner who had jumped was impaled on the top of what looked like an alien tree, they were in a forest of these strange outcrops for as far as the eye could see, dense, curling and tangled, they could see the light above but movement from where the bucket had set down was near impossible. The world outside the hermetically sealed dome was a very different one, far off noises could be heard, giant footsteps on the carpet sounded as if a huge beast were on the prowl, voices on the wind as Courage barked instructions in the distance, this was an eerie manmade world and the escapees faced as yet unknown dangers.

"Want to go back?", said one prisoner to the other,

"Not me, I'll take my chances," said the other,

and at that, one of the prisoners pulled some paper from his pocket and wrote,

'getaway vehicle gone, one dead here, escape impossible, abort'.

He placed the note in the bucket and in the next moment the bucket began to rise.

****

The two workmen left the building and made their way to their van which was parked directly outside.

"You did well today," said Hawthorne, *"But don't spook the customers, bent walls my ass,"* he laughed as they drove away from the nondescript building somewhere in New York.

"Fancy some lunch?" said Hawthorne,

"Yeah," said the other workman, *"I know a place, it's not far, I'll show you, take a left here."* They drove for a few minutes,

"Pull over here," said the workman,

"Jeez," said Hawthorne, *"Where can we eat around here?"*

At that moment the man pulled a gun from the door compartment of the van and pointed it at him,

"I'm going to need that toolbox," then bang, Hawthorne's blood splattered all over the driver's side window.

The man calmly picked up the blue box that was sat between them, got out of the van, walked a few metres to a car parked behind and got in.

"You got him?" said Sandy, who was sitting in the driver's seat of the car, *"Is he ok?"*

"Look for yourself, white box inside, be real careful," Sandy opened the toolbox and peered inside, a little white box with three tiny shapes within,

"Hey honey, is that you?" she whispered, *"You're free!"*

****

At the top of Green River 8, three more inmates rushed to get into the bucket, none noticed the note in the bottom. If everyone worked together, they had time for one more run, and at a push, possibly two. The bucket was again lowered into the abyss. One of the passengers noticed the note and picked it up, reading it to the others, panic ensued, they pulled on the rope, they shouted, but all to no avail, the bucket lowered at speed. Sometime later at the bottom they saw the dead man, and the other two escapees sitting close to the drop point.

"What the hell are you doing here?" said one,

"When we read the note, we were already on our way,"

"Well, we better make sure they don't miss it this time."

A few minutes later the bucket rose again, this time with two notes in plain sight. It was just 10 minutes before the end of yard break when inmates at the top discovered two notes, one describing the hopelessness of their situation and the other describing what they had found, they quicky decided that the best use of the last run was to send down some tools, a few shanks were thrown in the bucket, some water, a book of matches, and it was lowered for the final time. At the bottom, the five escapees grabbed for the contents,

"It's better than nothing," said one and then the silk thread began to fall, trapping one of the men's legs beneath the ever growing, ever widening pile,

"Move," shouted one, *"They've dropped the rope."*

The silk thread thrashed everywhere for a few seconds as the men tried to find cover until finally it was over, as the other end dropped to the floor, another of their number dead, crushed beneath the weight of 2,000ft of silk. At the top of Green River 8, the huge rubber plug was put back into the end of the needle, it would be a further three hours before they were due back in their cells and the nine inmates would be discovered missing by the guards. Conversation turned to the predicament of those below and all wondered if Wolf had made it out.

27
CARPET JUNGLE

The reports had arrived as expected and Millie and Elspeth poured through the information they had, there was a lot. First, they compiled a list of each facility Jimmy had been into and then cross referenced it against any local news reports in the vicinity of each of the care homes. The list of care homes numbered six and the two decided to investigate anything in chronological order.

"Look at this," said Millie, *"Another shooting, another woman,"*

"Yeah, but I've looked at the map and the incident is nearly half a mile from the care home," said Elspeth.

"Yeah, true, but we have the exact time from two separate witnesses who heard the gunshot, so it would be easy to check out."

Elspeth agreed, the two then focused on planning for the jump. The professor joined them, and they told him what they had found and what they were going to do.

"*Ok,*" said the professor, "*But I think we should not be telling Jack what we have so far, not yet, he's not himself, and I'm worried.*"

They all agreed but conceded that they would have to tell him soon, after all, they were a team and none of the three were comfortable about keeping things from the boss. The professor helped with putting the plan together, and they were glad for this. He was meticulous, and he always thought of every eventuality.

****

Warden Courage was preparing to leave for the day, it has been a good shift, he thought, longer than usual but a seamless swap out, and a gassing. Just as he was getting ready to go the comms crackled into life.

"*Warden Courage, we've got a problem,*" as a red light began to shine above the dome of Green River 8.

"*What do you mean missing, how many, have you looked everywhere?*".

"*Yes, we've followed everything to the letter, there are nine including Backman, and they are just not here.*"

"*Not there, what do you mean not there?*" shouted Courage as beads of sweat began to appear on his brow, this was just not possible.

Warden Courage hurried to his desk, flicked through monitors, until finally.

"*Control, this is Warden Walter P Courage, we've got a problem.*"

Yellow lights were then illuminated over the other domes, standard procedure, as all hell broke loose on the 13th.

****

Yellow lights flashed in Green River 5, Danny scuttled over to Millie, Elspeth and the professor,

"Back to your cells please, you'll be locked in tonight, now hurry, or I'll be for the high jump."

"What is it, Danny?" said Millie,

"A possible breakout on 8, unheard of, there are nine inmates missing so they are turning the place upside down trying to find them, now go, right now to your cells."

****

Warden Courage sat slumped in his chair behind the desk, how did this happen he thought, over and over, until he heard,

"Warden Courage, we've been sweeping the perimeter of the dome, we think we may have found something behind the benches at the basketball court."

Courage switched on the yard camera and zoomed in, he could see activity, guards, but nothing more. He got up from his desk and went over to the dome and peered in, still nothing, then on the outside of the dome he saw it, a tiny needle poking through the seal, back to his desk,

"Control, I've found the exit."

Courage sat back down, there was a procedure to follow, he

knew that, although he'd never done it, not even as a drill. Nobody ever thought escape possible from the domes. This must have happened on his shift, he had been there for nearly 10 hours now because of the swap out on 3, they must be down there in the carpet somewhere. They wouldn't have got far, and soon they would begin to grow and would be caught, he felt sure of that but, they did it on his shift, and there would be consequences. The comms crackled into life,

"Warden Courage, this is Control, please cordon off the area, we need a six-inch perimeter around the drop zone,"

"Roger that control," said Courage as he went to the desk drawer and pulled out a spray can.

He read the instructions carefully,

"Not more than six inches, spray glue evenly, ensure a complete circle," he mumbled.

He went over to the dome of Green River 8 and traced the needle down to the floor with his eye, there he saw a couple of tiny dots and some thread. This was it he thought, and he began to spray a six-inch radius of glue around the area, ensuring the circle was complete. Back at his desk, he reported the update,

"Area secure,"

"Thank you, Warden, you can step down."

Step down, he thought, step down, he never thought in a million years he would be told to step down but step down he did.

****

There were four men left alive in the shagpile jungle, one had died from his fall, the other crushed by the silk rope. The four watched as the giant figure bent over them and sprayed a substance all around.

"We can't stay here," said one,

"They know where we are now,"

"But it's impossible to get through this," said another as they began to panic.

"You got a better idea?" said a third and with that they began to move as best they could through the undergrowth.

"This will get easier as we grow,"

"Yeah but we'll be easier to spot, they'll catch us for sure,"

"Pipe down the pair of you, while they are looking for us, they're not looking for Wolf".

****

"Hey little guy," said Sandy as she looked at Wolf through a large magnifying glass at their safehouse somewhere in Harlem.

The plan was to hole up there until the new identities arrived for each of them. They were then to split up, head for the border, and meet on the other side.

"When you gonna be back to normal?" she said, *"You ain't no good to me as a little man,"*

"They'll start to grow after six hours from their last exposure, and another six and they'll be right. They've been out about six now, so you'll start to see a change soon," explained the workman.

"Jeez Rocky, Wolf's gonna be mighty pleased with you, walking him straight out like that, they all are".

****

Phipps sat at home in his chair, he had had plenty of time to think, he was off rotation because of the swap out, and wasn't due back in until the following day. He looked at the picture of Lucy, all the time wondering what he should do with his newfound knowledge. This was a dilemma, he felt certain he had been instrumental in helping the convicts to change the past, and he knew exactly why, details were still sketchy, but he knew why. His thoughts were interrupted by the telephone.

"Hello, oh hi Harry, what's up?", "Breakout?", Phipps heart sank, had he unwittingly had something to do with this, had he aided this escape?

"Oh, Green River 8, I see," Phipps breathed a sigh of relief, at least it wasn't 5, he thought.

He heard of the daring escape and that the escapees were still in his office. They would be caught for sure as soon as they started to grow, mind you, they had thought escape was impossible. Phipps also heard that he was to stand down, along with Harry, until further notice. Specialists were being drafted in to contain the problem.

"Specialists," said Phipps, he found this most amusing,

"Carpet cleaners, interior designers, ha, what do you do for a living?" he continued to himself, *"Well, my job is to look for criminals in your carpet!"* he laughed.

****

Warden Courage wasn't laughing as he sat in another office on the 13th floor being interviewed by two strangers about his shift that day. He recalled every detail including the swap out on 3.

"Decoy," said one man to the other,

"Maybe even the getaway vehicle," said the other.

"Get me the details of the two workmen on that shift," said the first into his telephone, *"Ok, I'll hold,"* as he waited with the phone to his ear.

"What is it?" said Courage,

"Well," said the first man, *"It's possible that these two were accomplices,"*

"Impossible" interrupted Courage, *"I've known Billy Hawthorne for 20 years, I know his family."*

The man with the phone spoke again,

"Ok, ok, I see, alright, get the report over to me pronto, and get an APB out on the other guy, although I'm sure that will turn out to be a false identity," the phone snapped shut.

"What is it?" asked Courage nervously,

"Billy Hawthorne is dead, he was found an hour ago on a quiet side

street in the city, it was a shot to the head,".

The colour drained from his face as Courage sighed and raised his hand to his forehead,

"And the other guy?" he asked.

The man replied with a serious tone,

"He's missing, we're going to need a description."

28
OPERATION SHAGPILE

Down on the office carpet the four men had made very slow progress. They had trudged through the shagpile, carefully climbing, and dodging until finally they reached the glue wall. Exit from here looked impossible.

"Don't touch that," shouted one of the convicts to another, but it was too late.

He put his hand against the wall, and it immediately stuck. A second inmate went to help him, but in the process, got stuck too, and the more they struggled the more they got attached, first it was their hands, then arms and finally bodies, they were going nowhere. It's everyman for himself thought one of the men, Zane, a lieutenant in the prisoners' hierarchy on the inside,

"I'm going to work my way around, to see if I can find a way through," he said, *"You go that way and do the same,"*

"Ok Zane, shout me if you find anything," as they parted company.

Zane moved as quickly as the circumstances would allow until he came across a hole that he thought big enough to crawl through at the bottom of the carpet where the glue had not dripped down. He felt a slight ache in his back, and he knew what was happening. He had heard of this before, he was starting to grow, which meant he was running out of time. Like a beetle on his back, he shimmied and wriggled through the hole to the other side and sat, weighing his options, then an idea sprang to mind. Zane began cutting long strands, with his shank, from these alien trees, touching them to the glue and then carefully attaching them to his body, first his torso, then the top of his arms and then finally the outside of his legs, until he was head to toe in a carpet camouflage.

****

"Permission to come into the women's quarters?" requested Danny at the door of the women's cells,

"Sure," shouted Millie, this was protocol.

Danny headed straight over to Millie's cell and told her the news of the breakout on 8, leaving nothing out.

"Wow," said Millie, *"And they're still there, in the office carpet?"*

"Yeah," said Danny, *"Although everyone's saying it's just a matter of time as they will start to grow soon, and the whole building on the*

outside of the domes is locked down tighter than a drum."

"But what does this mean for us?" Millie asked inquisitively.

"Well, security will be different up here, that's for sure, I'm supposed to lock you lot up every night now, so that privilege is gone, at least for now."

"Aw Danny, you run this wing, and you do a great job, surely you decide what happens on your wing, and anyway, how could I come see you when I want if I'm locked up in here?"

Danny coughed and went the usual crimson and quickly scuttled off.

"Go girl," chuckled Elspeth from the cell next door.

****

Specialised camera equipment had been put into the office of the Green River facilities and all attention was focused inside the glue perimeter on the floor. The cameras were a combination of normal surveillance and microscope equipment, with the ability to zoom in at very close proximity. The camera crew had already found the escape bucket, the silk thread and the two dead men at the drop zone. Attention was now focused on the area outwards to the glue wall, no thread of carpet left unexamined as the relentless search continued.

"There," said one of the camera operators to another as they sat in a room on the 13th looking at the screens. The operator zoomed in closer,

"There, you see," he clicked on the comms, *"We've found another*

two, they are alive, in the wall, they look like they are arguing,"

"In the wall?" came the voice back over the intercom,

"Yeah, they are up to their necks in it, they are not going anywhere,"

"Ok, that's four down, and five to go, let's keep looking."

In another room, two more guards were reviewing every detail of the recorded footage from that day's shift from the moment Wolf had entered the exercise yard. They saw him getting up from the benches, gathering with others and then he was gone, out of sight.

"That's when he disappeared, right behind the benches, switch to the office cameras,"

Within a flicker, they spotted it,

"There, movement on the seal at the top."

These cameras were much less sophisticated than those trained on the carpet, but good enough to establish a timeline, as all the pieces were slowly being put together. Elsewhere in the jungle, Zane struggled on, he was now about four millimetres tall and gradually progress was getting easier as he grew stronger, although it was tiring work.

****

"So, Warden Courage," the interviewer began, *"We have nine prisoners escaping under your watch, two confirmed dead so far, two more accounted for now so, that's five still at large. It looks like at least some of the prisoners escaped the building to who knows where, with*

the help of two workmen, one of whom you at least knew personally, so is there anything you would like to tell us?"

"You can't seriously think I had anything to do with this?" said Courage,

"Well, it doesn't look good now does it, why don't we go back to the beginning."

In the carpet surveillance room, the search continued.

"There!" said one of the men as they pointed to the monitor,

"We've spotted one more, he's moving around the inside of the perimeter, he has something in his hand, he's working his way around, looks like he's trying to find a breech,"

"Ok," came the voice from the intercom, *"Keep tracking him, the extraction team will be there in five minutes, I'll let control know, how big is he?"*

"He's about half a centimetre, hold on I'll get a precise measurement," *"Yup 5mm."*

"Roger that, stand by."

Within a few minutes the door opened, and a man entered wearing a dark blue uniform with K9 on a yellow badge on his shoulder.

"The dogs," said the first camera operator,

"Yeah," said the uniformed man, *"Where is he and how big is he?"*

"He's there," said one of the camera operators, pointing at

the screen,

"He has a makeshift weapon, and he's 5mm currently, we've just measured him, he'll be 6mm in 23 minutes."

"Ok," said the dog handler, *"I'm going in the room now, I'll need you to give me laser location two inches from the target, and well away from the wall,"*

"Ok, how many are you sending in and how big are they?"

"There are three Rottweilers, and they are about twice their normal size as far as he's concerned," and with that he turned to the door.

"Zoom out, laser ready," said one of the operators, *"Ok here's the handler, zoom in there, and laser on."*

A beam of light shone down onto the carpet from one of the cameras about two inches from the prisoner, the handler set down a small square of fabric to flatten the carpet and on it he placed a box, the box opened and three Rottweilers appeared, as the cameramen watched on in awe,

"Jeez, they are big," said one, as the beasts ran down the ramp and into the sea of carpet below.

In no time they had surrounded the prisoner on three sides, his back to the wall, growling and slavering as they got closer and closer, the man inching backwards until finally his back hit the wall, then an arm, he was stuck.

"How are we doing in there?" asked the handler from inside the office,

"He's glued to the wall,"

"Great," and with that the camera operators saw the man take something from his pocket, a whistle, he blew it, and immediately the dogs ran off in opposite directions.

Within moments the handler was back in the carpet surveillance room with the operators,

"Let's see now..." as he surveyed the screens, then speaking into a radio on his shoulder, *"One secure, the dogs are in the perimeter looking for others."*

"What next?" said one of the operators,

"Well, we'll sweep to see what we can find, after that, we'll widen the search. We only have three dogs and we don't have that much time left, they want them out before they get too big and start banging into tables," and with that, they all laughed.

****

"So, Warden Courage, they've found another, that's five accounted for, and four still missing. We are looking at every inch of the footage so if there is anything there, we'll find it. We've got a couple of officers turning over your apartment as we speak, so why don't you just make it easy on yourself, we will find out anyway."

"For goodness sake," started Courage, *"This is nothing to do with me, I've told you everything I know."*

"Ok, if that's the way you want to play it, let's go back again, tell us about the relationship with Hawthorne, exactly how long have you known him?"

****

Wolf was nearly twice the size as he was when he had arrived but still small, not even 1cm yet, and Sandy was beginning to get on his nerves.

"How's my little Wolfy then, my little, teeny weeny Wolfy, how's it going down there?"

She had been ribbing him for what seemed like forever, and he was losing patience, he shouted but she couldn't hear him, he was still too small and the music she was playing too loud. She swigged from a bottle of 808 single grain scotch and danced around the room as Wolf and his two gang members looked up at her.

"Hey, Rocky, let's dance," she shouted above the music, *"You are just my size,"*

"No thanks," said Rocky, *"Lay off the booze, we've only got to wait a few more hours until Wolf is you know, back to normal, and then we'll decide what to do,"*

"Normal? Paaaaa," hissed Sandy as Rocky moved to the radio and turned it off.

"I said, lay off it Sandy."

****

Back in the shagpile surveillance room, the handler and the two operators sat with the handler on his radio,

"The inside of the perimeter is clean, the dogs have been over every inch, do you want me to widen the search, control?"

"Roger that K9, we'll let them sniff around for an hour or so, the current thinking though is that four have made it out in the escape vehicle. The lab reckons there was room at a push, but it's worth a nose around,"

"Roger that, control".

The handler left and went into the office, blew his whistle, and scooped up the dogs. He took a small spray can and went over the glue with something, laid the box down again outside the gluey circle and blew his whistle. The beasts once again ran out in opposite directions, they were even bigger now.

"What was that you were spraying?" asked one of the operators, as the handler re-entered the surveillance room,

"That's to keep them away from the glue."

Zane battled with the jungle; he was headed for the door. In certain places he could see it if he climbed up one of these strange trees. He was under two feet away, or about a quarter of a mile at his scale, but the progress was still slow. He had carpet thread now tied around his arms and legs and he had fashioned a camouflage hat. Onward through the relentless forest, until finally he made it the door. He pulled himself underneath, hoping the other side would reveal an easier terrain.

****

"Now listen here Courage," said the interviewer,

"This is by no means over, you are now officially on leave, two weeks to start with, and we'll let you know how we get on, needless to say,

you are not to leave town, you can go now."

Warden Courage, exhausted by the cross examination, got up and left the interview room, and headed a couple of doors down the hall to his office.

"You can't come in here," said the guard standing outside, *"We have an operation running,"*

The door opened from the office he just left,

"Courage," the man shouted, *"Sit down right there, we'll get someone to escort you off the premises,"*

"What about my briefcase?" Courage shouted back, *"It's in my office,"*

"We'll get that back to you and, that's not your office anymore."

Courage sat crestfallen, in one of the chairs outside his office, where just a few hours earlier the workmen had sat. All the while he sat and waited for someone to escort him, what he didn't notice at this point was the tiny bit of moving fluff crawling up the holes in the back of his brogue shoes, like a hairy caterpillar, onto his sock and under his trouser leg. Within five minutes, Warden Courage, without his own knowledge, had helped another prisoner escape the building.

29
AN UNEXPECTED GUEST

It was Thursday and Phipps sat with Harry and Stella at their place eating ribs, and all conversation was about the breakout earlier.

"Couldn't happen to a nicer guy," said Harry,

"I feel sorry for him," added Stella, *"Imagine if that were you?"*

"Well neither of us are out of the mire yet," said Phipps. *"There's sure to be questions, and who knows how long this has been planned for, I did the paperwork and operations report for the swap out, and they reckon at least one of the workmen was an accomplice."*

The phone rang and Harry got up to answer it,

"These ribs are delicious," said Phipps to Stella as he licked his fingers and wiped his mouth with the napkin.

"Aw thanks Josh, we are always happy to have you over."

Harry returned to the table,

"You were right Josh, that was control, we both have to report in tomorrow for questions, Courage is on suspension, and we are being replaced on the Green River shifts until further notice."

"Are you worried honey?" said Stella to Harry,

"No," Harry replied, *"Me and Josh here have always run a tight ship, right Josh?"*

"Yeah, we sure have," agreed Phipps,

but he was worried, could this have anything at all to do with his terrible secret? Only time would tell.

****

Millie, Elspeth and the professor sat discussing the next planned jump, security was tight, but all of them felt it was possible to do the job quickly without detection.

"Ok," said the professor, *"The incident took place just under half a mile from the care home, it's unlikely Jimmy is the perpetrator so all you need to do is arrive, take the footage, and get back here as soon as possible."*

"And if it is him?" said Elspeth,

"Then we'll make another plan," said the professor. *"Now remember, things are different now, I've got to keep an eye on Jack whilst Danny and gods knows who else is keeping an eye on us in here, you need to be in and out, as quickly as possible."*

"Now," he continued, *"This mission is outside, so there are other variables like the weather that you have not had to deal with before. Satellite imagery shows a tree in the yard which has a good view over the area, so you should head there, but remember, the images are old, older than the incident, so the tree will surely have grown if it wasn't cut down. There's so much more to think about outside, so stay alert and keep your wits about you."*

"What else is there to think about?" enquired Millie,

"Predators" said the professor, Millie and Elspeth looked at each other.

"Hey, what are you guys talking about?" said Jack as he arrived at their table.

"Security honey," said Elspeth, *"Freddie here, thinks it's a good idea to stay clear of the sports hall for now until things calm down, and I agree with him."*

"Yeah," replied Jack, *"Good idea, I've been thinking about another jump, but we've got time up our sleeves, right?"* They all smiled and nodded.

****

Courage arrived back at his apartment and began to run a bath, he was exhausted. A ten hour shift and four hours of questioning, he would have a soak in the tub and get straight to bed. He undressed in the bathroom, threw his underwear in a wicker laundry basket in the corner of the room, and slipped into the hot water.

****

Wolf, Bull and Razor now stood about 3ft tall; they would be back to normal size soon enough.

"Hey Wolfy, why don't you come and sit on Mamma's lap," said Sandy,

"Knock it off Sandy," said Wolf.

He had been putting up with this for hours now, he was getting very angry.

"What's the matter little man, don't you want your Mamma to look after you? Now come over here and we'll watch some cartoons together,"

and at that Wolf moved over to a table, picked up a gun, walked over to where she sat, and shot her in the head.

Sandy slumped back into the sofa, lifeless.

"I told you to shut up," he said, then looking over at Rocky, *"Get rid of her."*

Wolf was a dangerous criminal with multiple murders to his name, and many more that they hadn't managed to pin on him. The four men knew Wolf well and they knew Sandy had pushed it, anyone of them would have gladly shot Sandy if Wolf had asked, he'd done the right thing, they all thought, she had disrespected him.

****

Courage stirred in the night, he got up and staggered sleepily into the bathroom, flicked on the light, and headed for the toilet. Behind him, he didn't notice the lid of the laundry basket lifting, as two eyes peered at him from behind, before the lid slowly lowered again. Courage finished his business, left the bathroom, and instinctively flicked off the light. However, another light from the kitchen down the hall partially illuminated the bathroom and the lid lifted slowly again. This time, a pint-sized man climbed out and followed Courage down the hallway to his bedroom, something in his hand glinting in the half light. Walter P Courage's body was found the next day when the two investigators visited to follow up on some more enquiries regarding the breakout, his throat had been cut with his own razor. The investigators wrongly concluded that Courage had been in on the escape, and someone had gone to his apartment to tie up loose ends. It wasn't until much later, forensics put forward the theory that, somehow Zane had made it back without the Warden's knowledge and had killed him in the night. This was supported by smaller than average fingerprints on the murder weapon and so Courage's name was eventually cleared. The breakout, together with mug shots of the criminals was all over the news; Sandy's body was found in a dumpster, and everyone was looking for Wolf and his gang.

****

Zane arrived at the safe house to the delight of the assembled gang members, Wolf sat on the sofa, Sandys penultimate resting place, as he slowly clapped Zane entering the room.

"Let's hope you weren't followed," said Wolf,

"I was careful," replied Zane, *"I like the new look,"* he said referring to Wolf's hair, which was previously long and dark, but now was short, spikey, and bleached blonde.

"Yours too," replied Wolf, referring to Zane's apparel - a three-piece suit, shirt, and badly knotted tie, all 'borrowed' from the Warden's wardrobe.

The five men sat around drinking beer and discussing their next moves. The mood was good, they were free men. Conversation turned to Green River 5.

"We heard they had built a flying machine," said Wolf, *"But how the hell would you fly out of there, Zane, you seen the outside, you got any theories?"*

"There's no way boss," said Zane, *"Maybe a part swap, but you would need it in the yard, in plain sight."*

"There's something more, something missing here," said Wolf,

"Those lot are all jumpers, it has to be that" said Zane,

"Yeah, and I know who will tell us," said Wolf.

"Hey Wolf, where's Sandy?" asked Zane, the other men looked edgy,

"She was here," said Wolf pointing to the empty space next to him on the sofa, *"Then she had to go,"*

"Oh well," said Zane, *"When you've got to go, you've got to go."* They all laughed.

"And you, Rocky, why were you in such a hurry to leave yesterday?" said Zane

"Ah, you know, you were late, and I had a pedicure," said Rocky. They all laughed some more.

30
AN OUTDOOR FLIGHT

Elspeth and Millie sat in the cockpit of the fly; they were ready to jump. The professor was keeping Jack busy with stories of the Second World War, and Danny was at his desk researching curling, a game where players slide stones along a sheet of ice towards a target – it was something Millie had expressed great interest in earlier. Dials were checked and double checked and THAWOOOO, the craft travelled back in time, to its pre-set destination, then the fall, the lights, the alarm, then steadiness as Millie brought things under control.

"There's the tree honey," said Elspeth, as Millie manoeuvred into position,

"Hold on, look down there," she said at once, *"Look the kid in the back yard,"*

"That's got to be him, it's the middle of the night,"

"I'll get in closer," said Millie, *"We need to be sure,"*

"Really honey," said Elspeth, *"I don't know about you, but where I come from, kids don't normally wander around in other people's back yards in the middle of the night."*

Millie circled the child at close quarters, it was Jimmy alright, and they watched as he picked up a stone and threw it at the window of the door at the back of the house. Another stone was thrown, then another until an outside light was turned on. In moments a woman appeared, stopped briefly, and then approached the child, she leant forward, her hands on her knees, only metres away from him, before he pulled a gun from his pocket and aimed it at her. She was smiling and put her hands in the air as if to surrender, she thought it was a game, but then there was a loud bang. Just as before, this woman slumped to the floor and was dead.

"Jeez," said Elspeth, *"He's got his own gun now,"* the boy took a few steps back, put the gun in his pocket, turned around, and calmly walked away.

"Let's follow him," said Elspeth,

"That's not in the plan," said Millie, *"We don't have time,"*

"Come on, just for a minute or so."

Millie obliged, and they watched as Jimmy crossed the field, into the distance and towards the care home.

"Ok I've seen enough," said Elspeth, her hand hovering over the jump button,

Suddenly and at great speed, a bird, swooped in front of

their windows, its open beak engulfing the craft,

"Jump," cried Millie, THAWOOOO, and they were back in the sports hall behind the mirror.

"That was close," gasped Elspeth as she unstrapped and went to the door,

"Take a look at this," she said, as they both peered out at the craft which was covered in gunge, *"Closer than we thought, this is bird spit!"*

****

Phipps and Williams travelled into the office together, both were to be interviewed by the investigators, so they waited outside an office on the 13th. A man poked his head around the door,

"Williams, you're up," Harry went in with a sombre appearance to face the questions. Phipps waited outside the office, time to think, he thought. What would he say if asked directly? They didn't know everything, how could they, he hadn't even pieced the whole thing together himself. No, he just had to keep calm, this was about the breakout, not about whatever had gone on a few days earlier, he would get back to Palmer in a day or so when he was back on rotation. The door opened, Harry walked out, and he looked ashen grey.

"Phipps," said the voice, and he got up as he watched Harry walk down the hall towards the shrink portal. Phipps sat in the office, waiting for the questions.

"So, Warden Phipps, how well did you know Warden Courage?"

"*Well,*" began Phipps, "*Not well at all really, we met whenever our shifts crossed, but we weren't friends, not like me and Harry, I mean Warden Williams. We spoke last a couple of days back on the shift change, and I prepped for the swap out on 3.*"

"*Yes, you saw the workmen the day before, anything there?*"

"*No not really, there were two guys, the first I recognised, he's been in the job a long time, although his name escapes me, but the other was a new guy.*"

"*Warden Courage is dead,*"

"*What?*" exclaimed Phipps,

"*We found him this morning, in his apartment, throat cut, we think he was an inside man.*"

"*Well as I say, I didn't really know him, but that surprises me.*"

"*Ok Warden Phipps, that will be all.*" Phipps got up to leave,

"*Oh, just one more thing, you were in conversation with one of the inmates on Green River 5, a Mr Jack Palmer for 40 minutes, what was that about?*"

Phipps froze,

"*I'm not sure I remember,*" he started, "*Er, it could have been any number of things, I generally talk to him about the prisoners on east wing, I can check the log,*"

"*No need that will be all, for now.*"

"*Do you know when Harry and I will be back to work?*" asked Phipps,

"You'll have your office back in a few days when they've finished in there." Phipps breathed a sigh of relief; he wasn't being sacked just yet!

****

Elspeth and Millie went straight to see the professor and relayed the events of the jump, including the close call with the bird.

"Probably a Nighthawk, they feed on the wing," said the professor, *"We'll get another camera fitted to the front of the cockpit, after it has been cleaned up".*

"We didn't hang around to check the colour of its plumage," said Millie, *"I'll get the craft cleaned up, but I vote we now speak to Jack."*

"I agree with Millie, there's much more left to investigate though, what do you think Freddie?"

"I think we have done quite enough jumping for now, that's three murders in just over two years, he clearly has a taste for this. There will be more for sure, Jimmy is a serial killer, and he's just getting started."

"But what about any other murders, shouldn't we be at least continuing to find out more?" said Millie,

"I don't suppose it will hurt to keep looking through the information we have, but no more jumping, you two ladies have had a very lucky escape. We talk to Jack about what we have so far, and it will be his decision as to what happens next," said the professor.

They waited for Jack to arrive and took him through every detail of what they had uncovered. Jack had this look in his eyes they had not seen before. He looked distant and cold, until finally he spoke,

"So you've all been snooping around behind my back, digging up the past, who the hell do you think you are?!"

"Now wait a minute," said the professor, *"There was no ill intention here, we are your friends, and we all thought it best to see what we could find out before speaking to you, there's much more, we are sure of that, but we all felt now was the time to speak to you, honestly Jack, you've been through a lot, and we all meant well."*

Jack paused for a moment, seemingly regaining control of his emotions,

"Ok," he said, *"but from now on, no more secrets."*

31
HERB

"Ok, lets saddle up," said Wolf as the gang headed for the door.

The five men clambered into an old van, Wolf and Rocky up front and three on the bench seating in the back.

"Is this thing hot?" asked Wolf,

"Yup, but I took it from long term parking out of town, and I've changed the plates so she'll be good for now," said Rocky, as he turned the ignition.

They were paying a visit to Smallz; they hadn't made an appointment. Herb was sitting at his desk when he heard some loud crashing from reception downstairs,

"What's he broken now," he mumbled, *"No not you sir, I will have to call you back, someone here has knocked something over by the sound of it,"* he replaced the receiver and stood up from his chair.

At that moment Wolf and two others walked in,

"Mr Backman, I wasn't expecting to see you," said Herb, *"How's he doing down there, nothing broken I hope?"*

"One of the boys is looking after him, nothing broken yet Herb, and you can call me Wolf."

"Well, you are quite the celebrity Wolf, you've been all over the news, I have to say, I'm impressed, first ever breakout from one of the domes, but what I don't understand is what you are doing here, it's a big risk, shouldn't you be lying low?"

"Thank you for your concern, Herb, but we'll manage just fine. Now I need you to tell me exactly what has been going on over there in Green River 5, and I mean everything."

"I run a business here Wolf, client confidentiality and all that, loose lips are bad for business in my game, you know that."

Wolf nodded at Zane, and he began to move towards Herb's desk,

"Now hold on, hold on, there's no need for any of that, gentlemen," said Herb, *"Why don't you take a seat,"* as he waved at the two seats in front of his desk, *"What exactly is it you want to know?"*

****

Jack and the Millie sat in the canteen,

"So what do you want to do Jack, you know we can't change the past, it's too long ago, and I'm not sure what we can do now, we only have Jimmy's movements up until he was 18, we've no idea of his whereabouts after that."

170

Jack thought for a moment,

"I know where he is, at least I knew where he was six years ago when I came in here."

"Wow," said Millie, *"How come?",*

"Well, I lost contact with him when we were both about 13, but when I was doing quite well in business, I paid a private investigator to track him down. I was going to get back in touch after I'd jumped back to see what had happened."

"And?" enquired Millie,

"And I started to make journeys back, not just the farm, but other places too, and I got clumsy, I got caught and I ended up in here."

"So where is he, well, where was he when you last tracked him down?"

"Well," Jack began, *"When he left the care system, he joined the forces, like me and others, it was a natural progression after you'd been in care, and like me he got his wings, he left the forces, spent some time as a pilot privately, flying internationally, and then went into the leisure industry, last I heard he was Resort Director at The Palomino,"*

"What the little one?" said Millie, *"Yeah, just out of town on the E190."*

****

Elspeth was sitting with the professor as he was fitting a camera to the front of the craft:

"So, Freddie, since I own the only Lanthaneodinium mine in existence, I thought I'd ask about it, what's the deal with the audio recordings and why are the cockpit video recordings always in black and white

and keep it short please?"

The professor smiled,

"Well, it's all to do with EMI, Electro Magnetic Interference, the molecules in the Lanthaneodinium get agitated by the movement of the craft, this causes the video and audio to be distorted, if the craft were to be stationary for a short while, the quality of audio and video would improve dramatically."

"And what's so special about Lanthaneodinium?" said Elspeth,

"Now the answer to that one is very long indeed," said the professor.

"Ok honey, I get it," Elspeth conceded.

"Let's try this thing out," said the professor as he tapped the newly fitted camera, *"This will record automatically every time we jump, now go switch on the monitors in the cockpit, you'll see quality is much improved as this thing hasn't moved in a while."*

In the cockpit, Elspeth flicked some switches, and the monitors sprang into life,

"einigkeit und Recht und Freiheit, fur das deutsche Vaterland." as the professor sang the German national anthem from outside the craft, Elspeth switched everything off,

"Yup quality of audio and video much better, but there is a problem,"

"What's that?" said the professor,

"The quality of the singing honey," they both laughed.

32
ELVIS

Wolf and the gang sat around discussing the information Herb had given them earlier at Smallz.

"So, they've built something that flies, that we know," said Wolf,

"We also know they had outside help, apart from Herb and his crew, but who was that guy in the video we saw at Herbs office, the guy with the miniature case?"

"I know that guy," said Rocky, *"Why didn't you say?"* said Wolf,

"I didn't want to say anything in front of Herb, he sang like Elvis when we spoke to him, we didn't even have to hurt him none."

"Fair enough, but who is he?"

"That's one of our Wardens, I saw him the day before I got you guys out, well most of you," he looked at Zane, and Zane looked back,

"Pedicure my ass," said Zane.

"Ok knock it off, you guys," said Wolf.

"Want me to go and rough him up some, see what he has to say?" said Rocky,

"No," said Wolf, *"Won't need to, he helped them for a reason, we just need to know what that reason is. Bull, you and Razor find out exactly who he is and where he lives, keep an eye on the place, speak to one of our guys in the police department, they'll help, we pay them enough."*

"I'll bet you any money that weren't no radio they smuggled in neither," said Zane,

"No, it was not," said Wolf, *"Who's hungry? I know I am, I could eat a whole Warden."*

33
THE PAST IS OVER

Phipps was pleased when he heard he was allowed back into the office. He still needed to speak to Palmer about all of this and he still wasn't sure of all the details, or even what he would say. But what if he just ignored it, left everything as it was, what was his gain for digging up the past? Digging he thought, that rings a bell. Then there was the core reason, Lucy, he didn't want to go back to a different before, one where Lucy was not there. His thoughts were quickly interrupted by the telephone.

"Hey dad,"

"Hey, is that my lovely daughter?" he said,

"I need a favour, can you have Lucy overnight tonight, somethings come up, short notice, and I need a sitter, can you help?"

"Sure, it will be my pleasure, is she sleeping over, I'm back to work tomorrow so I can drop her off at school if it helps?"

"That would be great Dad, I'll be over in an hour, and Dad?"

"What is it my love?"

There was a pause and then,

"I had a terrible nightmare about her the other night, it was awful,"

"Well don't tell me" said Phipps, *"You'll give me nightmares too, best not to tell anyone really, happens sometimes about the ones we love, it's because you love her so very much,"*

"I do dad, and thanks, thanks for everything, you know,"

"I know, see you soon." Phipps put the phone down.

It was best not to tell anyone he thought, he knew what the nightmare would have been - he had had it himself, only the nightmare was not a nightmare, but a different version of the past. That was it, he had decided, he was going to forget about all of this, as if nothing had happened, and it would all be behind him, it was done now, and very soon, it would all be a distant memory.

****

Millie went to find Elspeth to share the information she had been told by Jack.

"Good work Millie, so I think we've got another job to do now," said Elspeth,

"But Freddie said no more jumping," replied Millie.

"Who said anything about jumping, I think we should pick things up at The Palomino and find out if Jimmy is still there, I can go back to

my contact and see what he can dig up, he'll have a social security number, a driving licence, this is good Millie."

"And what about Jack, he'll be upset if he knows we're snooping again?" said Millie,

"Don't worry honey, I'll see what I can dig up on the quiet and we'll only use it if we need to."

"Did Jack say what he wanted to do, another jump, or anything else?"

"Not yet, I guess he'll let us know when he does, but Freddie has now got the Bayze and the radio casing in his cell, so there will be no jumping without express permission from Herr Friedrich von Shultz."

"Ok, I think you should continue to work on Jimmy's time in the care homes, I'll get my contact to pick up at The Palomino, and I think the four us need to sit down soon and talk about when the hell we are getting out of here."

****

Bull arrived back at the hideout with information on their target.

"Well, his name is Joshua Phipps, he's been in the prison service for 25 years, he has a good reputation there and is an upstanding member of the community. He looks after a kid, took her to school this morning, we are working on her name, we followed them there and then Razor followed him into work before heading back to the school for the pickup later."

"Ok, thanks Bull," said Wolf, *"What we don't know is why he's been helping them, who runs things over there?"*

"Palmer, Jack Palmer, well he runs the east wing, there's only a few of them over in that wing, all jumpers," said Bull,

"And what about Herb's nephew, what's his name?"

"That's Willie G Patterson, but he won't know any more than Herb, and I think Herb told us everything he knew," said Bull smiling.

"Ok," said Wolf, *"We'll speak to this warden first, then we'll get a message into Palmer via Willie. Who do we know in the kitchens on 5?".*

"I'm on it," said Razor, pulling out his phone,

"How do we get to the Warden?" said Wolf,

"He eats in the same place every morning," said Bull, and at that moment his phone rang.

"Hey Razor What's up?" "Ok, ok, I'll let the boss know," and he snapped his phone shut,

"The kid's name is Lucy, we'll have her address later, she's his granddaughter."

Wolf smiled, the plan was coming together, he relished the thought of a warden working for him, this was going to be fun.

****

The next morning in the canteen, Elspeth was talking to one of the serving staff and then went straight to Millie,

"He's still there," she said,

"Who's where?" enquired Millie, unsure of what Elspeth was referring to.

"Jimmy, he's still at The Palomino, goes by the name of Jay,"

"You sure its him?"

"Yeah, one hundred percent honey, I've got my guy seeing what he can find out about what he was doing before then, but Jimmy, Jay, it's him."

"Ok, we tell Jack straight away, no secrets,"

and they resolved to speak to both Jack and Freddie as soon as possible, to discuss the future, and the past.

34
THE GAUNTLET

Phipps sat in his same spot in the deli, Mary had served up the usual and he sat eating as the customers thinned out. Phipps spotted a man at the other end in a booth staring at him, and when there were only the two of them left in the place, the man approached and sat opposite him.

"There's plenty of space in here," said Phipps, but the man just sat and stared,

"Excuse me sir, I'm minding my own business here, why don't you move to another booth." The man sat silently, so Phipps got up,

"I wouldn't do that if I were you Warden," said the man, Phipps froze, then slowly sat back down.

"What do you want?" said Phipps.

"The boss wants to see you," at that point Mary appeared,

"Is everything ok Josh?"

"Yes, fine Mary, just fine," and she turned and walked away.

"And who is this boss of yours?" said Phipps trying to stay calm, but under the table his hands were shaking,

"Oh, you'll find out,"

"Well, what if I don't want to find out?" Phipps said nervously,

"Well," said the man, leaning forward now, *"That would not be wise now would it, there would be consequences, you see."*

"Oh, consequences," Phipps mumbled, now more distressed than ever but still trying to stand his ground.

"Well consequences for you of course, but also for Lucy," said the man.

"What?" whispered Phipps angrily, *"If you have so much as hurt a hair on her head, I'll…"*

"You'll what?" interrupted the man, *"Call the police? I don't think so, see that van across the road, you're going for a ride, now pay the check, and go get in the back of the van."*

Phipps did as he was told, and as Mary watched from the counter, he left deli, the man remained in the booth, now staring at Mary, until she left for the kitchen at the back. Phipps opened the door to the back of the van, and there in front of him was Wolf. Phipps recognised him immediately from the monitors at work and the news coverage of the breakout,

"Warden Phipps, come in, so kind of you to meet me,"

he looked over his shoulder as Zane closed the doors

behind him,

"Let's go," and the van pulled off.

****

"Willie G wants to see you," said Elspeth as she passed Jack in the hallway,

"What does he want?" said Jack,

"I don't know, I didn't ask, but don't forget the four of us are sitting down this morning,"

"I didn't forget, I'll go now to see what he wants," and with that Jack headed off to the kitchen, and Elspeth to the games room to see Millie and the Professor.

They were sitting in front of the tv, and the news was blaring out regarding the breakout a few days earlier. Nobody yet arrested, but the commissioner was promising all resources necessary for their imminent capture.

"Where's Jack?" asked Millie,

"He'll be here soon, he's just got to go see Willie in the kitchens, have you told Freddie the latest about Jimmy, Jay?"

"Yes, she has," said the professor,

"What we need to discuss when Jack gets here is how and when we are going to get out of here," they all nodded. Jack joined them a few minutes later.

"We've got a problem," he said as he sat down.

"*Has this got something to do with Willie?*" said the professor,

"*Yes, well no, he's just the messenger, apparently, but that guy wants to talk to me,*" he said as he pointed at the TV showing a mug shot of Wolf Backman.

"*Jeez,*" said Millie, "*That can't be good, what it's all about?*"

"*I don't know*" said Jack, "*But whatever it is, you are right, it can't be good, we'll find out soon enough.*"

"*Now honey,*" Elspeth started, "*Jimmy is still at The Palomino,*"

"*I see,*" said Jack, "*More skulking around behind my back?*"

"*Now hold on honey, if this were behind your back, I wouldn't be telling you now, would I? Anyway, it's something for you to think about, we all need to discuss our next moves, and when we are planning to get out?*"

"*Yes,*" said the professor, "*This is important, but I would like to make a jump or two of my own,*"

"*Where?*" said Millie,

"*I'd like to go back to a couple of historic events in the Second World War,*", they all groaned, and at that moment,

"*Palmer to the communications room, five minutes.*"

"*I better see what he wants,*" said Jack as he got up to leave, "*We'll reconvene when I'm back.*"

Jack sat in the communications room waiting for Phipps to speak, Phipps sat in his office wondering what to say. Phipps eventually broke the silence,

"We've got a problem, I had a visit,"

"Ok," said Jack, *"Tell me everything,"*

"Well one of the escaped convicts, a Mr Backman, has been in touch with me."

Jack's worst fears realised, he decided to say nothing regarding his conversation with Willie G until he knew more.

"So, what did he say?",

"Well, he's a bit of a crazy guy, you should see his file, he mentioned something about a flying machine, that bit's nonsense I know, but he did mention time travel, and he did mention you."

"Tell me more," said Jack,

"Well, he's serious, he knows where I live and he knows where Lucy lives, he said if I didn't help there would be consequences, well the other guy did, but he means business, that's for sure."

"Yes, but what does he want?" said Jack losing patience now.

"He said he would be back in touch, but didn't say what about, said he would be speaking to you, has he spoken to you?"

"No," said Jack, a half-truth, *"I'll take care of Wolf,"*

"Oh, so you are on first name terms then?" said Phipps,

"No," replied Jack, *"He's been all over the news, I've seen it on tv, try to stay calm and get back to me as soon as he is back in touch with you, and we'll take it from there."*

"Calm?" said Phipps, *"He's threatening my family,"*

"Look," said Jack, *"You have to keep it together, wait until he is in touch again, don't do anything stupid, and I will handle this, Ok?"*

"Ok," said Phipps, define stupid he thought, *"But what are you going to do?"*

Jack sighed, *"Do you really want to know that?"* then Jack got up to leave, he was heading to the kitchens.

****

Wolf and the gang sat back at their hideout plotting.

"So, do you think that whole flying machine thing is just a rumour Wolf? The warden didn't know nothing, and he would have to, hard to hide an airplane inside,"

"I don't know," said Wolf, *"But they have got a time machine, that much we do know, and that's all we need."*

"Hey fellas, remember that rumour about a spider inside the dome on 7 who ate half the prisoners?" said Zane,

"Yup, I remember that," said Wolf, *"And folks believed it too, for a while".*

A phone rang and Wolf pulled a mobile from his pocket, he looked at the screen,

"Well looky here, it's Elvis," they all laughed as Wolf took the call.

"Hello Herb, I do hope you're not still all shook up," the gang sniggering like kids in a playground,

"And don't gimme no jailhouse rock," more sniggers, Wolf was a big Elvis Presley fan.

"Now start talking, we all got suspicious minds here,"

Wolf listened for a few minutes intently and then snapped the phone shut.

"Well, I'll be," he said, *"Jack's going to meet me on the outside, he says, he'll let me know where, you got to admire his balls,"*

"Anything else?" said Rocky, *"Says he's going to need a few days to set it up,"*

"Well if we're meeting on the outside, they got a time machine that's for sure," said Rocky.

"What if it's a trap?" said Bull, *"What if he just turns us in?",*

"He can't do that, we have information, and we have the warden," said Wolf smiling, *"We all sit tight for now, and we keep tabs on Phipps."*

35
SERIAL HELP

Jack went back to share the news with the others, he knew he had to enlist some help if he was to pull this off, he would discuss it with the team, and they would agree a plan.

"It's worse than expected," said the professor, *"They've got to Warden Phipps, how's he holding up?"*

"Well, he's shaken, but I think he will be ok for now. I've sent a message to Wolf to say I will meet him in a few days, so that will buy us some time."

"But how can you meet them, Jack?" said Elspeth, *"They'll be back to the usual size, that's not a fair fight,"*

"I've been thinking about that, I think we need to enlist the help of Jimmy."

"You mean the serial killer?!" said Millie, *"The one who we have witnessed killing three women in cold blood for no reason, and god knows how many more since then, you mean that Jimmy?"*

"Look..." began Jack, *"I don't see we have a choice here, and remember, he doesn't know what we know, not yet,"*

"And do you think he will help?" interrupted Elspeth.

"I don't know but I think we have to ask, a meet in The Palomino would work, at least from our perspective," said Jack.

"I have to agree with Jack," said the professor, *"Jimmy is not the most ideal of partners, but we are not spoilt for choice. Warden Phipps is the wild card here, he doesn't exactly fit the bill as a criminal mastermind, and although we dealt with him in a polite and professional way, somehow I think this Mr Backman will not afford him the same courtesy."*

"So what do you propose?", said Millie,

"We need to get a message to Jimmy asking for help, and I will need to go to meet him,"

"There's no 'I' about it Jack, it's we from now on," said the professor, *"If he agrees to help, and if we can find a way to arrange a visit to The Palomino in a giant fly, then Millie will go with you and can get you out if anything happens to you, agreed?"*

"Agreed," said Millie and Elspeth.

"There's no other way Jack," said the professor, *"Agreed?"*

"Agreed," said Jack reluctantly.

"Ok so we are all agreed, Elspeth, you and I will work on the jump parameters, Jack you will prepare a note for Jimmy, and we'll send that out in the usual way, Millie you will get the craft ready for the jump."

"Are the kitchens not compromised now?" said Millie,

"*No, it will be business as usual,*" said the professor, "*and if it does go astray and falls into the wrong hands, all Jack is doing is asking for help to set up the meeting, we'll work on the second part of the plan when we know we can achieve the first. Ok let's go to work, we don't have much time.*"

****

"*How are those fake ID's coming along Rocky?*"

"*They will be here this week, they're clean too, the real deal, social security numbers, driver's licences, even passports,*"

"*Good work Rocky.*"

"*Passports?*" said Zane, "*Where you off to Rocky? Wherever it is, you'll be leaving early,*"

"*Real funny Zane,*"

"*Knock it off you two, now let's take a look at those plans.*"

"*So how is this going to work Wolf?*" said Zane as he rolled out some drawings of The Union National Savings Bank in New York.

"*Well,*" said Wolf, "*It's simple, once we get our hands on the time machine, we'll go back a few days and rob the bank,*"

"*And if it goes wrong?*" said Bull,

"*Then we'll jump back and do it again, and again and again, until we get it right,*"

"*That's genius boss, and what about Palmer, what about the warden?*"

"Well, we won't need either of them once we've got the machine."

****

"Can we speak privately Freddie?" said Elspeth,

"Sure Elspeth, what is it, you look worried?"

"I don't know where to start really," she paused, *"I guess I've not been totally honest with you, well with all of you really,"*

"go on…" said the professor,

"It's about The Bayze,"

"What about it?",

"It's not the only one, there are others."

"What?" said the professor, *"I thought there were only seven in existence until you told us about the eighth?",*

"Well yes, there are more, two more to be precise, on the estate,"

"But how, why?" said the professor in disbelief.

Elspeth went on to explain that Harrold was a significant shareholder in Bayer Zeit Losungen, the company that developed and manufactured the Bayze. He was given shares in exchange for Lanthaneodinium supply and also a seat on their board. Harold arranged for three extra machines to be made, one for himself and two for the Saudi's as they were unable to develop their own machines with the Lanthaneodinium he had supplied to them on the black market. He was caught for the illegal supply, but not for the production of the additional machines, all buried in the grounds of the estate.

"So why are you telling me all of this now?" asked the professor,

"Well," began Elspeth, *"Do you remember a while ago in one of our time travel lessons, I asked you if I could see me, if I travelled back in time to a place where I knew I was previously?",*

"Yes, I do,"

"Well there was a reason for that question."

"Continue," said the professor, a mixture of fascination and worry,

"Just after Harold died, god rest his soul, and the day I was arrested, I was sitting in the garden, it was a beautiful day, I was drinking homemade lemonade under the shade, then from the treeline not far from me I saw a woman, I was shocked at first, but she waved at me and smiled, stood for a moment and then disappeared back into the woods. It lifted my mood and I didn't know why, but what I do know is that it was me Freddie, me waving at me."

"And you are sure it was you?"

"Without a doubt, not then but after you and I spoke, and since. Freddie, I think I need to go back to the estate, and get another Bayze, the thing is, I don't know why yet."

The professor thought for some time about this new information,

"Well, this is something you cannot tell the others, I understand why you have told me, but not the others,"

"Why?" said Elspeth,

"Because it may influence their actions in such a way that we disrupt the event, the present, and indeed the future, we must wait now Elspeth, all will become clear in the fullness of time." Another pause, *"I do wonder why that day specifically though,"*

"I've thought about that," said Elspeth, *"I had just lost Harold and I was very low, I was worried about the future, but here I am, and with all my new criminal friends, I'm the happiest I've been since then. Perhaps in the future I'll decide to go back to let me know everything will work out just fine, and seeing that woman lifted my spirits back then, I knew I could deal with whatever life had to throw at me."*

"It's a lovely story Elspeth and thank you for trusting me with it, I will keep it safe, for all our sakes."

The professor made his way to see Millie, to work on the flight parameters, they had not yet heard back from Jimmy, but it wouldn't be long before they knew one way or another and they needed to be ready to go at a moment's notice.

"Ok Millie, I've had a look at the layout of The Palomino, and I think we will land in here, its separate from the other buildings, it is a sports hall, just the same as ours, only bigger, and it has a basketball court."

"Tell me Freddie, why are we taking the craft in, why don't we just take the Bayze and go on foot?"

"I thought of that," said the professor, *"But this is too risky, I want you in the cockpit when Jack speaks to Jimmy, Jimmy doesn't know what we know, but there's no telling how Jack is going to react when they are face to face, and if anything does go wrong, you jump, don't even think about it, under no circumstances are either of you to leave the craft unmanned, not for a single moment."*

"Do you not trust Jack?" said Millie,

"I do, but can you honestly say how you would react when you knew what Jack knows? The situation is a volatile one, and so we must treat it as such and take every precaution."

"Ok," said Millie, *"So what's next?"*

"You go through the usual checks as you would normally, so we are ready to fly, but we won't be starting the engines, we are going to jump from here to there and back again, the mission time is 7 minutes."

"No flying?" queried Millie,

"No, we will need to get Jimmy to ensure the space is empty at around the time we will be there, that will be the next message we send out if he agrees to the meeting, now let's go find the others."

Millie and the professor joined the other two in the games room,

"He's in," said Jack.

"Good," said the professor, *"We need to get another message to him regarding where we will meet, Millie will take you through that when we have finished here, now Jack let's go through what you are going to say to Jimmy."*

"Ok," said Jack as he cleared his throat, *"Well, it's been many years now since we both met, we'll do the pleasantries and then I'll explain our problem,"*

"Do you think you can keep it together Jack?" said Elspeth, *"That won't be easy, surely?"*

"I've got no choice," said Jack, *"We need Jimmy's help, and as I said*

before he doesn't know what we know, he has come this far, whether or not he'll agree to help us out with the problem we have with a gang of ruthless murderers is another matter!"

"Well perhaps there's some sort of murderers code, and he'll side with them," said Millie,

"Come on honey," said Elspeth, *"I don't like this anymore than you, but we really don't have any choice."*

"Ok then, its settled," said the professor, *"Millie you now need to brief Jack on the jump zone parameters, Jack get the message out to Jimmy and go see Phipps, its time he took some leave, we'll get a message to Mr Backman, once we know Jimmy is in for stage two. If he isn't, we'll need to move to plan B",*

"Plan B?" questioned Elspeth,

"Yes," said the professor, *"I'll work on that, if I need to."*

The team looked at him, they all knew Jimmy's help was fulcrum, they really needed him.

36
UP TO HER NECK

Elspeth made her way to see Danny,

"Can I have a word please Mr Maguire, in private?"

"Sure Mrs Braithwaite, and you can call me Danny when the others aren't around."

Danny liked Elspeth, real classy he thought, she probably shouldn't even be in here.

"Come down to my office, we can talk in there," he said as he led her down the hall.

"So, Mrs Braithwaite, what can I do for you?"

"Well, I need to speak to the Warden,"

"It's Warden Phipps today," said Danny.

Elspeth already knew that.

"Can I ask what it is you need to speak to him about?"

"Well it's rather a delicate matter," she began, *"I would really like to speak to him in person,"*

"I can get you an appointment with a nurse in the infirmary, if that helps?" enquired Danny.

"That's very kind Danny, but I'd like to have a word with the Warden first,"

"As you wish," said Danny, *"I will effect an introduction immediately."*

Danny was putting on his best voice, after all Mrs Braithwaite was a lady,

"I'll call him directly," he continued, and with that he picked up the telephone.

"Very good Warden Phipps, I'll let her know, he will see you now, in the communications room,"

"Thanks honey," she replied with a sweet smile, and she was gone.

A real lady he thought, he did hope she was ok. Elspeth sat in the communications room waiting for Phipps. The team had thought too many visits from Jack to see the warden would arouse suspicion. Phipps looked at Elspeth, she couldn't be mixed up in the Backman affair, he thought, he had picked something up from her estate, but surely, she had been coerced into that.

"Mrs Braithwaite, what can I do for you?" he said finally.

"We are working on your problem," said Elspeth abruptly.

She was up to her neck in it, he thought,

"Please continue," he said.

"You are going to book me an appointment in the infirmary when we have finished, that will be the reason I am here to see you,"

"Are you unwell?"

"No," she continued *"But in half an hour, you are to complain of a stomach ache, and then it will worsen to the extent that you have to leave work within the hour, You are then to head directly to The Columbia University Medical Centre, do you know where that is?"*

"Yes," he confirmed.

"Good, you must then ask to speak to a Doctor Alan Sinclair, he will diagnose suspected appendicitis, and you will be booked in for immediate surgery."

"Surgery?" questioned Phipps, *"But there's nothing wrong with me?"*

"We know that, but that is what will happen, and don't worry, there will be no surgery, you will stay in overnight, and the doctor will recommend two weeks convalescence, he will let you know where."

"But why, what's going on?"

"Now listen here warden, we are all working very hard here to ensure the past we have created for you remains intact, failure to comply, and the whole thing falls like a house of cards. You do like the way things are, don't you?"

"Yes," replied Phipps,

"Then you best get on and do as you are told."

Beneath that charming veneer was a tough, resourceful, smart woman and at times, just the right amount of scary, if you got the wrong side of her.

"Do we understand each other Warden Phipps?"

"Yes, we do," he replied,

"Very good," and with that she got up and made her way to the infirmary.

****

Wolf and the gang were busy, Wolf sat on the sofa, looking at the fake ID's,

"These are good," he said,

"Yup, they're real too, they are in the system," said Rocky, *"You get pulled over, and even if the lawman knows you are the famous Mr Backman, first man ever to escape the domes, you'll come up cleaner than your mamas apron."*

"I never knew my mama," said Wolf as he tossed them to Zane,

"Who came up with these names?" said Zane, looking at the documents,

"They're mostly dead people," said Rocky, *"But all real clean,"*

"Good work," said Wolf.

Bull and Razor were on stakeouts, Bull keeping tabs on

Phipps while Razor was outside Lucy's school. The phone rang,

"Oh, here he is," said Wolf, *"Elvis is in the building,"* they all laughed as Wolf picked up the phone, holding a finger up to his lips to hush his audience.

"Hey Herb you old hound dog," giggles, *"It's now or never,"* more giggles then a pause,

"Oh ok," more serious now, and then finally, *"Well there's no point returning that to sender."*

There was raucous laughter as Wolf snapped the phone shut.

"What is it Wolf?" said Rocky,

"Well, it seems the meeting is being organised, we are on, at The Palomino,"

"What the little one?"

"Yup,"

"I don't like that boss," said Zane.

"No, I get it," said Wolf, *"I never expected Palmer to come see us all shrunk, but I also didn't expect us to get down to his size."*

"I've got a bad feeling about this," said Zane,

"Let's sit tight for now," began Wolf, *"He won't know we've got Elvis on the payroll, let's wait 'till we hear from Palmer."* The phone rang again,

"Elvis?" said Rocky giggling,

"No it's Bull," *"Hey Bull, ok, you follow him, don't lose him and call me back when you know where he's going and what he's doing,"*

"What is it Boss?"

"Phipps has left work early, Bull is on it." *"Viva Las Vegas!"* sang wolf loudly, the other two joined in.

37
THE OPERATION

Phipps pulled up in a cab outside The Columbia University Medical Centre, and at reception asked to speak to Doctor Alan Sinclair.

"Just a moment," said the receptionist,

"Ah Doctor, there's a Mr...?"

"Phipps," said Phipps,

"Mr Phipps," said the doctor as he approached the desk,

"We've been expecting you," as he led him down the hall. *"Abdominal pain?"*

"Er yes," said Phipps, as he was led into the doctor's office.

"Jump up there," said Sinclair as he closed the door behind them.

"You know why I'm here?" said Phipps,

"Mr Phipps, I know why you are here, it is because you have abdominal pain,"

he's actually going to examine me, thought Phipps,

"But by the look of you I would say it could be appendicitis," he looked at Phipps right in the eye.

"Yes, yes," said Phipps, *"But you are the doctor",*

"I am the doctor, and I'm afraid we will have to operate immediately, it's quite a simple procedure, you'll be in overnight and then a bout of recouperation. Ok, you can get off of there now, just wait in the hallway, someone will be along to get you ready for theatre,"

"But you are not actually," started Phipps,

"Come come Mr Phipps," interrupted the doctor *"No time like the present."*

In no time at all a nurse came and led Phipps down to a room to change into a gown,

"You are not actually…" Phipps stopped, *"Never mind,"*

"Any questions should be directed to Doctor Sinclair, I'm just here to get you ready for theatre," said the nurse. *"Now I'll be waiting out here, for when you've changed."*

A few minutes later, Phipps was on a bed, being wheeled to theatre. He looked worried, the nurse left and in a few moments Doctor Sinclair appeared.

"Now Mr Phipps, if there's not a problem we will not need to operate,"

he winked, but what did that mean thought Phipps.

"Now we'll put you under, then I'll have a good look,"

"Put me under?" exclaimed Phipps as the doctor put a mask over his face,

"Now count to 10,"

"Under?", repeated Phipps,

"That's right, 1,2 come on," *"1,2,3,4..."* and he was out cold.

****

The message came back from Jimmy at the Palomino, two words, *always empty,*

"That's good," said the professor,

"Ok, Jack, Millie are you ready?"

"Ready as we'll ever be," said Millie,

"And you Jack?"

"Yeah, I'm ready,"

"And Jack..." said the professor,

"I know, I know," said Jack, *"I'll be fine,"*

"Ok, then let's roll," and with that, Millie and Jack clambered into the craft.

"Elspeth," said the professor, *"Get an urgent message out, a simple one. Jack when you get there you will need to wait, we'll expect you*

when we see you, there's no telling how long it will take for Jimmy to receive the message, allowing for our different time coordinates, roll call here is in 45 minutes, you abort after one hour, whether or not the meeting has happened, are we clear?"

"Crystal," said Millie.

"Oh, one thing more," said the professor, *"There will be a slight drop when you get to the other side, I couldn't calculate how deep the flooring was and I didn't want to risk the legs being embedded in the floor, that's about a 3ft drop,"*

"Roger that," said Jack.

Millie and Jack sat in the cockpit ready for the jump, prechecks complete, dials turned to just 30 minutes before the timeline they were leaving, THAWOOOO, and the sports hall was empty once again.

"It's in the lap of the God's now" said Elspeth, *"I'll get that message out pronto."*

Jack and Millie landed inside one of the sports halls of The Palomino Beach Resort, Spa Hotel and Golf Course, and with a bump, Millie unstrapped and headed out of the craft.

"You wait here," she said, *"Professor's orders, just one of us out at any one time. I have to take dimensions to finesse the professor's calculations for the next jump here. If there is a next jump here, I reckon we can take at least two feet off the drop."*

"Ok," said Jack, *"Well we've got to wait a while, Jimmy won't even be getting a message for the next 30 minutes, I've set the clock, we abort in T minus 59 minutes,"*

"Roger that," said Millie as she checked her watch.

****

The phone rang in Wolf's pocket,

"Jeez, it's Elvis again," he said, *"Hey Herb,"*

"Ok, ok," Wolf listened intently, he wasn't in the mood for fooling around on this call.

"Ok, so what did the first message say again, not that one, the very first message. Ok, thanks," and he snapped the phone shut.

"What's up Boss?" said Rocky,

"Two more messages, one out says 'always empty', and one in says 'here', damned if I know what that means."

"Boss," pleaded Zane,

"Pipe down Zane, we have to wait to hear from Palmer, nothing's changed, we know he's arranging a meeting, and we know that's in two days, he doesn't know we know, so we wait, at least for now, see what he has to say."

****

It was T minus 22 minutes to abort, when the sports hall door opened,

"Show time," said Jack,

"I'll give you some privacy," said Millie, as she turned down the audio speakers in the cockpit,

"Thanks," said Jack, he paused for a moment before

continuing, *"Millie, I'm glad and lucky to have you as a friend,"*

"Ditto" smiled Millie, *"Now go out there and give him hell, I mean not hell, I mean, you know, get the job done,"*

"I know what you mean," said Jack as he chuckled and clambered from his seat and left the craft.

Millie eyed Jimmy, she could see the likeness, they were mirror images of each other. Jimmy was looking bemused at the giant fly in his sports hall,

"Yeah, you look," said Millie, *"You're gonna get yours soon enough,"*

she placed her hand close to the jump button as Jack approached his brother, they embraced.

"Way to go Jack," she mumbled to herself, *"Good start."*

The brothers walked together closer to the craft as they talked.

"Not in here," said Millie as she reached for a makeshift blade she had at her side *"Prepare to repel borders,"*

Jack was waving his hands at the craft in an animated way, just like a salesman selling a new car, she thought. They walked away and Millie breathed a sigh of relief, this was stressful she thought. The whole time they conversed she kept one hand over the jump button, watching as they continued for what seemed like an eternity. A bleep in the cockpit bought her attention back to inside the craft, it was her watch and she flicked on the comms,

"T minus five,"

and she saw Jack look at his watch, she could see him wrapping up the conversation.

"Come on Jack, got to jump soon," she said under her breath.

Finally, another embrace and Jack was back inside the cockpit, Jimmy watching from the door.

"He's gonna love this," said Millie as Jack strapped in, *"Ready?"*

"Ready,"

and THAWOOO, right in front of Jimmy's eyes the craft just disappeared.

Back in their own sports hall, Elspeth and the professor saw the craft arrive,

"Good days fishing?" asked Elspeth as they got out.

"Yes," said Jack, *"It went well, it was good we had longer than the original plan of 7 minutes, that would not have been enough,"*

"Ok, well done both of you," said the professor, *"Full debriefing in the canteen, let's say 30 minutes, I want to have a look at those parameters of yours Millie and make the necessary alterations, I'll join you there,"*

and with that the three of them left the professor to fiddle with things in the cockpit.

****

Phipps woke up in a hospital bed, in a private room. His head was foggy and he felt drowsy, to his left, he saw a sorry looking bunch of flowers, and beyond those, the nurse he had seen earlier, sitting in a chair.

"Ah Mr Phipps, you are awake, I'll get the doctor," and with that she left the room.

Within moments she was back, this time with the doctor in tow. The doctor picked up a clipboard from the end of the bed as the nurse reported,

"He's on analgesics through IV, opioids to supress the pain, hydromorphone, he's nil by mouth until the morning and his vitals are just fine,"

"I see, thank you nurse, that will be all for now," and the nurse left the two of them alone.

"How are you feeling Mr Phipps?"

Phipps went to sit up but was immediately hit with pain in his stomach,

"I was fine when I walked in here, what have you done to me?"

"Well, Mr Phipps, we had to take your appendix out,"

"What?" hissed Phipps, *"There was nothing wrong with my appendix,"*

"Well…" the doctor continued, *"You came in here with acute abdominal pain, I thought it was a burst appendix, so I had no choice but to operate,"*

"Now listen here," said Phipps angrily,

"No, Mr Phipps, you listen here, your appendix, or lack thereof, is the least of your concerns, you don't need it, even now we doctors don't

really know what they do, I had mine out when I was five years old and I've been as fit as a fiddle ever since. And anyway, you have other concerns."

"Oh really?" said Phipps, he moved to sit up, but the pain was more acute now, so he laid back down.

"Yes," the doctor continued, *"Your nephew was asking after you, very concerned, he left you those,"* he pointed at the flowers,

"A bit old to be a nephew of yours I thought, a bit rough around the edges too, tattoos, a sleeveless denim jacket, but he obviously cares, he's still sitting out there waiting for an update," he peered through the window blinds, to the road outside.

"So you just decided to operate on me when there was absolutely no need to do so" protested Phipps,

"Now Mr Phipps," said the doctor assertively, *"Whatever kind of muddle you have got yourself into is no concern of mine, as far as I am concerned, I have carried out a successful operation to remove your appendix, and your medical records will say as much. But if you left here with your appendix, the medical records would not be correct, and that would come back to me,"* a pause, *"Now then,"* he said more softly, *"Shall I go see your nephew and let him know you'll be in overnight?"* Phipps nodded reluctantly.

"Very good Mr Phipps, now it seems you have a benefactor, and you will be leaving here to convalesce tomorrow at some point. There will be a car waiting to take you, there's another exit out the back, but more on that after you have rested, I'll go and put your nephews mind at rest," and with that the Doctor left.

Phipps laid back on the bed, contemplating life without his

appendix.

****

The professor joined the others for the debrief in the canteen, and to discuss their next moves, he looked very worried.

"Everything ok Freddie?" said Elspeth,

"Yes fine," said the professor, *"Millie a great job with the dimension parameters, I've altered the trajectory very slightly to arrive two feet lower, so there will barely be a bump this time,"* *"Ok,"* he continued, *"What was agreed with your brother Jack?"*

"Well," Jack began, *"I have agreed with him that we will be back there at the original date we set, that way if our messages were intercepted, Backman will think all is well, so we have two days to prepare, and Jimmy has said he will help in whatever way he can, he gave me this number so I can make direct contact,"* Jack put the number back in his pocket.

"Ok," said the professor, *"It's decided, we'll get the message out to Wolf, this time I think we'll do it by telephone. Also, Elspeth, can you get the doctors help there?"*

"I think so honey,"

"Good, and how is the patient?"

"Well, there were complications, they actually had to operate,"

they all looked at Elspeth in disbelief,

"Phipps was being tailed," she said, *"The guy is still there, obviously one of Backman's crew, actually came in and started asking questions,*

said he was his nephew, the doctor took the decision to make the whole thing more real. I think it was the right decision, for everybody,"

"Maybe not for Phipps," chipped in Millie, *"Good job it wasn't a fake amputation,"* they all smiled.

"Ok," said the professor, *"So getting the phone to Wolf will be easier than I thought, let's keep Phipps in for another day or so, problems with the op or something,"*

"I'll let Sinclair know what he needs to do," said Elspeth.

"The thing I'm struggling with here," said Jack, *"Is that Backman and his crew are going to take the Bayze, even if – and a big if – we manage to set them up to get caught, we'll lose the time machine, they will make sure of that,"* the professor shot a glance at Elspeth,

"Let me have a think about that," he said, *"I'll come back in a day or so with some theories,"*

"Oh yes," said Elspeth, *"I may need to jump to see the doctor,"* this was her cover story for an entirely different journey,

"Oh yes of course," said the professor, *"Of course you will, Millie can go with you, we'll discuss that Elspeth after we've finished here,"*

"I can do the jump," said Jack,

"No," said the professor, *"I need you here to go through these game theories, we need to work out a way to keep that Bayze."*

****

It was the next morning and Phipps lay in his hospital bed, the nurse plumping pillows, and when the doctor walked in, the nurse left.

"Good morning Mr Phipps, how are we feeling?"

Phipps thought for a moment,

"Well considering I've undergone surgery for something that was not necessary in the first place, I'm feeling a bit peeved,"

"Now, now Mr Phipps, there's no need for any of that, this arrived for you," he said, setting down a box with a mobile telephone in it. *"Perhaps your nephew needs a phone, he's outside the room, he'd like to see you, I've told him you will be here for another day or so due to complications with the op, we're going to keep you in to keep an eye on you."*

"Complications?" said Phipps nervously,

"Yes," said the doctor, *"Don't worry though, no more surgery, shall I send him in?",*

"If you must," said Phipps reluctantly.

The doctor left and within moments Bull entered the room and slammed another bunch of flowers down on the table, this bunch sorrier than the last,

"How you doing Warden?",

"I've been better, they are keeping me in,"

"I know, me and the doctor are real friendly, what's this?"

"It's a telephone, it's for you,"

"How'd you get this?"

"I don't know, ask the doctor since you are so friendly, I didn't nip out

to the shops, in case you hadn't noticed, I've just had surgery."

"Ok Warden, I'll take that," and he turned around and left.

In the hallway he bumped into the doctor, he waved the box,

"Yes," said the doctor, *"It was left on reception today, I didn't know it was for you until your uncle told me, now he'll be in for at least another day, possibly two. I'd like him to get as much rest as possible, of course you can visit though whenever you want,"* and with that he was gone down the hall.

38
ELSPETH'S JOURNEY

"So this is it," said Elspeth, *"It was all leading up to this,"*

"Yes, it seems so," replied the professor, *"Now as far as anyone here is concerned you will be landing in the doctor's bedroom six years ago. We of course know differently, from this timeline you will be gone from here for a matter of minutes, your own personal journey much longer, I estimate approximately 15 hours. The second jump is planned for exactly 16 hours after the first."* The professor paused, *"I've placed the tube in the craft already, you will rest in that until you are big enough to fight off any predators."*

"Is that really necessary Freddie, we know I survived until I was fully grown as I saw myself in the garden that day,"

"Yes you did," said the professor, *"But who's to say that tube didn't actually save your life in the early stages of your travel, and I am trying to think in a way that I would, had you not shared information*

with me previously."

"The tube will grow with you," he continued, *"At the same rate until you are about an inch tall, so when it starts to get a bit tight in there, you'll need to get out, you'll then be big enough to fend for yourself. There's also a weapon in the tube, a large needle, same rules apply, it will grow with you until it reaches full size, at two inches tall your growth rate will start to accelerate quite dramatically. You've said there were blankets on top of the wardrobe, you'll use those as cover until you are big enough to climb down."*

Elspeth listened intently and nodded along as the professor went on,

"I've put some fabric in the tube which you can wear to save your blushes until you are fully grown, you'll have your own clothing in your room so you can change into something more suitable when you are full size, everything clear so far?"

"Yes," said Elspeth nervously, *"I think so."*

The professor considered her for a moment,

"Ok, so then you will go to the garden, make sure nobody sees you, and retrieve the Bayze, you must wait until you are arrested, well the other you, and then make your way to The Palomino, how are you going to do that part?"

"Harold has a collection of cars at the back of the property, I'll take one of those and drive there."

"Ok, so we are all set. Elspeth, I am so worried about this mission, there are too many variables, so much could go wrong,"

"Don't worry Freddie", she interjected, *"It's my destiny, and*

anyway, I'll be back in a couple of minutes."

****

Bull arrived back at the hideout unaware he had been tailed. He took the box straight to Wolf, who emptied its contents, put in the sim, turned the phone on and tossed it on the table in front of him. Vintage mobile phones had been used by the criminal underworld for some time, more advanced communication tools used by most, but these, sometimes unreliable mobiles, ensured conversations could be had without the authorities listening in. They waited, until finally the relic rang.

"Who's this?" said Wolf as he opened the phone,

"Jack Palmer," was the reply,

"Mr Palmer, I've been sitting here on my sofa waiting to hear from you, you took your time."

"I needed to get things organised for a meeting on the outside, thought you'd prefer that to a prison visit,"

Wolf laughed, *"Oh you know, they're not so secure these days",*

"Yes, so I hear," said Jack, *"Congratulations are in order."*

Wolf smirked before continuing the conversation and getting straight to the point,

"Ok, where and when?" He of course knew the answer to both those questions, but he didn't want to give the game away.

"Well," said Jack, *"Given our predicament in here, we thought it best to meet on equal terms, so I'm going to say The Palomino,"*

"The little one? Yup, I know it."

Jack gave details of the person they should meet on arrival to ensure they had no difficulties getting in.

"How do I know you are not going to double cross me?"

"You don't," said Jack, *"But I've got something you want, and we have no use for it once we're out of here, I'll tell you more when we meet but we've planned an escape of our own."*

"Ah," said Wolf, *"The time machine, well you better make sure you bring it."*

"I'll bring it, but there is one more thing," said Jack,

"Go ahead," said Wolf,

"You leave Phipps and his family alone, the machine will give you the power to go anywhere at any time, you'll be the most powerful criminal in the world,"

Wolf smiled; he liked the sound of that.

"And why don't you want to be the most powerful criminal in the world Mr Palmer?"

"Oh, you don't think we've been busy over here in 5? We're all set up; we have everything we need, and when we get out of the dome, not only will they be wondering where we've gone, they'll also be wondering when in time we've gone, they'll never find us." Jack thought that sounded good.

"Ok," said Wolf, *"We're set."*

"Ok," said Jack *"I have to say Wolf, you did a great job getting out*

of 8, I admire the work."

With that, Wolf snapped the phone shut, he liked Jack he thought, a good partner, still he would have no qualms about killing him if the circumstances demanded it.

****

Millie and Elspeth were preparing for the jump,

"What's the cargo?" said Millie,

"That's my coffin," said Elspeth referring to the large transparent tube.

"What?" said Millie,

"Just kidding honey, it was the professor's idea, we're landing on top of a wardrobe, and I've got to wait it out until I'm full size so that's where I'm sleeping. At least to start with until I get a bit bigger, don't suppose I'll get a wink though,"

"Why do you need to see the doctor?" said Millie,

"That part's classified," said Elspeth, *"Freddie's orders, I don't know why but I trust there's a good reason, something to do with variables on the possible outcomes."*

"What?" said Mille,

"I didn't understand it either honey, you know how it is when he gets started with all his time travel theory. One thing's for sure, there'll be more of all that before we are finished here."

"Ok, let's do the pre-flight,"

"Roger that,"

"Ok, that's a roger go on co-ords,"

"That's a roger go on time," Mille paused. *"Six years ago?"*

"Honey, let's focus here,"

"But Elspeth…"

"Millie, enough already, we are a roger go for the jump, repeat a roger go for the jump."

THAWOOO! And they were gone, falling, alarms, lights then steady again as the craft was under control.

"Ok Millie, you are going to set her down up there, let's do a sweep first,"

"Roger that," as Millie swept the area on top of the wardrobe.

"Dusty, he needs to have a word with his cleaner," said Millie,

I do thought Elspeth.

"Look," said Millie *"Over there in the corner, spider web,"*

"Yeah, we'll get as far away from that as possible honey," said Elspeth nervously. *"Ok, set her down here."*

Millie and Elspeth unloaded the tube from the craft, along with some fabric and a needle, which was more like a spear from their perspective. The needle had a makeshift handle around its middle, like a javelin would.

"You expecting trouble?" asked Millie,

"Better safe than sorry," began Elspeth, *"Now when you get back Freddie will be jumping with you to pick me up, and all being well you'll see me in a few minutes. Now don't be giving him the third degree about times and locations, I want you there on time, not a second late, understood?"*

"Understood," said Millie, as they hugged,

"Come back safe," said Millie.

Elspeth smiled and set the timer on her watch - 16 hours and counting. THAWOOO. Not even a second later, and she was all alone. Elspeth dragged the tube to rest alongside some blankets at the top of the wardrobe. I wondered where that had gone, she thought as she touched some silk at the bottom of the pile, she clambered inside the tube, covered herself in the fabric, spear by her side, and settled in for the long wait.

****

Just after the craft had been created, the professor and Freddie chose a location for the team's safe house, a derelict building right next to JFK, they spent time monitoring it, and it had been deemed suitable. The plan was to ship the team back to one week before they escaped, this would give everyone enough time to get back to full size and go their separate ways before they were discovered missing. Jack and the professor had been briefing everybody one by one and a departure date had been set. Each of them had been given 20 million credits on preloaded cards. It was a significant sum, even in the 22nd Century. This was of course courtesy of the Elspeth Braithwaite Estate; false papers were also provided, and the only stipulation was that each must leave

220

the safe house one by one and travel by air to an international location of their choosing. If any of them wished to get back in touch with their family or friends that was up to them, and they did so at their own risk. Lastly, any discussion about the aircraft they had built was forbidden. Bob Gosling limped up to Jack, still wearing his plastic boot,

"Hey Jack, I'm impressed, to be honest I never thought you'd pull it off,"

"Well we haven't yet Bob, but fingers crossed. Have you thought about where you'll go? You know you don't have to tell me, actually maybe it's better if you don't."

"No, I trust you Jack. It's Venezuela for me, sun sea and sand, I got a load of money parked down there from before coming in here. It's going to be paradise, I'm going to find a wife and live like a king."

"Sounds great Bob,"

"When do we go Jack, and where are you going?"

"Both classified my friend, but be ready to go at a moment's notice".

39
HIDEOUT SPY

As soon as Millie arrived back in the craft, the professor clambered in,

"Are we going to pick up Elspeth?" said Millie,

"No," replied the professor, *"I have a very important mission for you first, give me that flash drive and put this new one in, it has enough memory for what we need,"*

Millie did as she was told.

"Now come here little one." He had never called Millie that before, but she quite liked it. *"You are going to Wolf's hideout,"*

"What?" said Millie, *"How do we know where it is?"*

"Elspeth had one of the gang members followed, anyway that is not important, now listen to me carefully".

"I'm listening," said Millie, as the professor began to explain,

"Watch what I am doing," as he knelt by the Bayze, *"Four cables red, green, yellow, blue, all colour coded, these link directly to the dials in the cockpit,"* as he pulled them out one by one. *"Next the fibre optic at the top,"* as he turned a large metal collar, and pushed the fat pipe away, *"One more clip and out it comes."* The professor pulled the Bayze from its holding and set it aside.

"Now this switch on the side is called the boomerang switch, we never use it but just so you know, it locks two sets of coordinates, you can't use the dials, and you can only move from one place to another and back again. Now put it back together please."

Millie did as she was told and slowly put everything back together again

"Now out, that's good," and finally, *"Back in again,"* Millie followed instructions and did the job well.

"Why?" Millie began,

"Questions, questions little one, now please listen carefully". *"You are going to fly the craft to the location, we are travelling back to 30 minutes before Wolf received the call from Jack, that will be enough time for the Lanthaneodinium to settle and audio and visual will be good, the front camera records automatically. It's a disused warehouse so there is plenty of room to fly around inside. Wolf mentioned a sofa, find it and then, find a suitable place to land where you have a good view of the sofa, once you are in position you will take the Bayze from its casing as I have shown you and Jump back here."*

"Why don't I just stay in the craft and wait?" said Millie.

"No, there are too many variables. Instead, you will walk 50 paces from the craft and jump back here. I will be waiting, we will reset the

time, adding 2 hours, and you will jump back and reverse the process, are we clear?"

"I think so," said Millie,

"You must know so," said the professor, looking very serious now.

"I know so," said Millie,

"Good, now when you get back to the craft if it is compromised in any way whatsoever, you must return with The Bayze. If it is not, then all the better, now it is time for you to go, good luck." And with that Millie strapped in and the professor left the craft.

This was her first solo flight, so she was very careful to check each of the dials again and again, there was simply no room for error. THAWOOOO, and she was gone.

Within no time Millie had returned with the Bayze,

"Excellent," said the professor, *"How was it?"*

"All to plan," said Millie,

"Ok let me see the Bayze," he rolled the dials, *"All set, off you go, hurry back."* and off she travelled again.

The professor waited, until finally Millie arrived back in the sports hall, the craft intact. The craft had been in the gangs hideout for a full two hours but Millie had managed the whole mission in a matter of minutes on their timeline. The professor clambered in,

"Well done, well done, now let's take a look at that video," as he played with the dials on the dashboard.

****

Phipps was on his feet in his room, he was a little sore but feeling better physically, although still mourning the loss of his appendix.

"Ah up and about Mr Phipps, that's good," said the doctor as he entered the room. *"You'll be leaving in the morning, on your way to convalescence, The Palomino, it's very nice,"*

"What, the little one?" said Phipps,

"Yes, that's the one," said the doctor, *"It's very nice, I spent time there with my wife actually, there's so much to see and do, now take this number, you must book this yourself, on your own credit card,"*

"But what about my benefactor?" asked Phipps grumpily,

"You are to be reimbursed I hear, also you are being upgraded to the presidential suite, everything included, phewee," he whistled, *"How fancy."*

The doctor looked dreamily into the distance, contemplating a presidential suite at The Palomino,

"Now," he said finally, *"The car will be here for you at 10:00am, I'll make sure you are all checked out, for your departure from here, and when you've finished with your booking I'll need that card, you must settle with us."*

Phipps was really grumpy now,

"It's you who should be paying me," he grumbled under his breath,

"Sorry Mr Phipps?" enquired the doctor,

"Nothing," said Phipps, and with that, the doctor was gone.

****

"But when are we picking up Elspeth?" said Millie,

"All in good time," said the professor.

"You fetch Jack, and we will all watch the flight recording together," and with that Millie set off and within minutes the two were back in the craft.

The professor had queued up the video to the point at which Wolf picked up the phone to Jack sometime earlier.

"Who's this? Mr Palmer, I've been sitting here on my sofa waiting to hear from you, you took your time. Oh you know, they're not so secure these days. Ok, where and when? The Little one? Yup, I know it. How do I know you are not going to double cross me? Ah, the time machine, well you better make sure you bring it, go ahead, and why don't you want to be the most powerful criminal in the world Mr Palmer? Ok, we're set," and with that, Wolf snapped the phone shut.

In the craft the three travellers watched on as Wolf leant forward over a set of plans.

"It's The Union Bank," said Jack as the three listened intently to the conversations between Wolf and the gang.

"So that's it, they are going to use the Bayze, in trial and error until they get the job right," said the Professor,

"It seems so," said Jack, *"I think we can offer them a more solid idea but, in every scenario, we will lose The Bayze,"*

"Let's worry about that later Jack," said the professor, *"For now we must concentrate on offering them a plan that is more finessed, a plan that works for us too."*

40
THE SPIDER

Phipps was in a limo on his way to The Palomino and, six years earlier, Elspeth was preparing to get there herself, just after the resort had opened for the first time to customers. All night she had seen the giant spider patrolling its area, around from behind the blankets, marching past her every 20 minutes or so, trailing a sticky web from its abdomen, she didn't sleep. At one point a light in the room came on, then another in the bathroom and Elspeth had a chance to view her surroundings, she saw the webbed work, nothing touching the tube, but strands all around her like a glistening fence. Elspeth couldn't see past the top of the wardrobe, but she knew it was a giant version of herself preparing for bed. She remembered back then, just after Harold had died, she always retired early, in the hope of some rest, she was in mourning, Harold, for all his faults, had been a good husband. Eventually the lights were turned off and Elspeth found herself once again in a thick cloak of darkness.

She didn't see the spider again for the rest of that long, long night, but she felt its presence, and as dawn broke, she felt her back aching, this was it, she was starting to grow. As the light became brighter in the room, she could see her surroundings properly, soon she must pull herself from the safety of her capsule and face life on the outside. She waited as long as she could, it was time.

"Come on honey," she mumbled, as she pulled herself free from the tube, wrapped in fabric, spear at hand.

First job, she thought, was to see where her neighbour was,

"Do spiders sleep during the day?" she said as she walked slowly to the edge of the blanket pile, peering around gingerly.

There it was, inches from her face, big, brown, with a tawny coat of hair. Eight black eyes, like inky dots on its head, four facing forwards and four more looking above and to the rear. Elspeth, moved slowly back behind the cover of the blankets, and then very slowly peered around the corner, but this time the spider was gone. All she needed to do, she thought, was hide until she got a little bigger. All around her Elspeth saw spider web, she was trapped, there was no way out, she held the spear in both hands ready to defend herself. This is it she thought, it was her time, she was ready to go down fighting. And then all at once she heard a voice,

"Elspeth Braithwaite, do not be alarmed, this is Commander Briggs of the Spider Ship Orb 16"

Elspeth froze. What was she to do?

Again, a voice, *"Elspeth Braithwaite, this is Commander Briggs, do not be alarmed."*

Was she going mad?

"We are here to help you, please do not be alarmed,"

she peered around the corner once more and again the spider had appeared.

"Hello Elspeth, we are here to help."

Was the spider talking to her?

"Breathe," she said to herself,

"Yes, you must breathe," said the spider.

"Who are you?" asked Elspeth nervously,

"My name is Commander Briggs, we are here from the future, a research ship, tracking your story back to its origins,"

"What story, and what origins?", demanded Elspeth.

****

"Welcome Mr Phipps," said the receptionist at The Palomino Resort, *"Your room is ready for you, it's The Presidential Suite, we do hope you have a comfortable stay, your luggage will follow shortly,"* and with that another staff member appeared.

"Welcome Mr Phipps, have you ever been shrunk before?" Phipps groaned.

"Ok then, so please follow me."

Phipps did as he was told and before long the two of them

had arrived at a large set of double doors.

"Now Mr Phipps, this is where the magic happens and this is as far as I go, this is The Presidential suite entrance to the resort. When the doors open, you must step inside, these doors will close behind you and another set will open, step through those and you will see a single chair."

"Single chair?" enquired Phipps,

"Yes, a single chair. You'll need to sit in that, and as soon as you have, we'll do the rest,"

"And when will I get shrunk?"

"As soon as you sit down sir, it's that simple, we'll be watching all the way, anything else sir?"

"I guess not,"

"Then enjoy your stay at The Palomino sir," and with that the first set of doors slid open.

"Thank you," said Phipps.

As he stepped through, they closed behind him, and another set opened to reveal a single white leather lounge chair. It was a beautiful piece of furniture whatever your taste. Phipps stepped through the second set of doors, and considered the chair for a moment, a concave white wall before him with the seat facing it. He slowly sat down. When's it going to start, he thought, so he sat a little longer but nothing. What should he do? He looked over his shoulder but there were no doors behind him, perhaps he had already been shrunk? Then all of a sudden, a whirring noise, very quiet to begin with, but slowly getting louder and louder. Phipps looked ahead of him, on the wall there appeared to be a tiny dot, a dot getting bigger as the whirring got louder, until he could begin to see a shape. Bigger still, until into his view came a black hovering limousine, pink neon lit from underneath, it slowed as it approached until finally, it was there, a door opened, and a man got out.

"It's ok sir, you can get up now, I'm your driver to The Palomino, it's a 3 mile journey, we'll be at your suite in 30 seconds."

Phipps got up from his chair and walked slowly to the hover limo, I could get used to this he thought.

****

Elspeth sat, now more comfortable with her new eight-legged friend,

"So, you are saying you are from the future, you have been tracking our story back, and you are here to help me?".

"Yes," said the commander from within the ship, *"But I can't tell you any more than that I'm afraid,"*

"I know, I know," said Elspeth, *"The professor told me about not saying anything in certain situations, but what I don't understand is why you are here in the first place, won't that change the future in some way?"*

"We're getting better at that, we've run the numbers, and it's good all round if you complete this part of the mission, there's certain things we can now do for the better."

"Ok," said Elspeth inquisitively, *"But"?*

"*There's not much more I can say,*" said the Commander, "*Except this, you must never discuss this encounter with anyone, never, not even the professor, this must go to your grave with you, lives depend upon it, do you understand what I am saying?*"

"*Well, I can keep a secret,*" said Elspeth boldly, she could, and she would.

"*Are you at least allowed to tell me what would have become of me if you weren't here?*"

There was a long pause.

"*Ok, there were two other outcomes before this, in the first scenario, there was an actual spider, you killed it after a long and brave fight, but were fatally wounded. In version two we arrived, you had a really good go at us, damaging the ship, but fell to your death from the wardrobe, and this, this is scenario three.*"

Another long pause,

"*Well then I guess I ought to thank you guys for being here,*" said Elspeth.

"*Mrs Braithwaite,*"

"*Call me Elspeth,*"

"*Elspeth, some things can't be explained, and some things must not be explained, for example, six years ago when you lay in bed down there in the dawn light, could you have possibly imagined that a tiny version of yourself would be talking to a spider on top of the wardrobe?*"

Elspeth snorted with laughter and slapped her thighs; a giggle came from within the ship,

"And can I at least know your name?"

"That can't hurt, my name is Ryan, Ryan Briggs and it's a real pleasure to meet you. Now we've got to get you down off this wardrobe and under the bed, you'll stay there until you are ready to leave, everything has been prepared, and we'll stay with you for the first bit."

"Ok," said Elspeth, *"What do you want me to do?"*

****

Jack, Millie, and the professor sat discussing the plans they had heard the gang making earlier.

"Their plan is a crude one, but you have to admit, it just might work, why do you think they will go for ours?" said the professor.

"It's because they will see ours as safer for them, more likely to succeed, and they only have to execute it once," said Jack *"They have no travel experience so we have to assume they will take one of us with them and I think that one person will be me."* There was a pause.

"Not necessarily," said the professor.

"What do you mean?" said Millie,

"Well, what if Jimmy would agree to pose as Jack?"

"What?" said Millie, *"You mean the serial killer Jimmy, that one?!"*

"Please Millie," said Jack, *"None of this would have been possible so far without him, and as we have said, he doesn't know what we know about him. If you give him any inclination that something's off, you are going to endanger the mission and all of us with it. We have to put that aside for now and we'll deal with things when the time comes,"*

"And when will that be?"

"We'll know when the time comes." said the professor, *"Millie, it will help greatly if you just think of Jimmy as you would Jack and put the rest out of your mind for now, if it wasn't for what we know, we would think of Jimmy in that way, things would not be at all possible without his help"*

Millie slumped back in her chair and folded her arms.

"Do you think Jimmy will agree?" said the professor.

"All we can do is ask," said Jack, *"He's helped us so much to date, he knows my circumstances and that has not put him off. In fact, he knows we are all illegal travellers and nor has that. Asking him to spend 12 hours in the company of four dangerous murdering fugitives on the inside of a giant safe might be a bridge too far".*

"We still can't get past our problem though, can we?" continued Jack, *"In every outcome we still lose the Bayze, and then there is the additional problem of getting everyone out before we lose it."*

"Well," said the professor, *"There is some good news there, I have managed to hack the video feed to our wing which beams to the outside. I've been recording our comings and goings for some time, so we can loop a stream of activity which will buy us some time there, Danny is still a problem of course, he will see we have gone."*

Both Jack and the professor looked at Millie.

"What?" she said.

41
THE PRESIDENTIAL SUITE

"Welcome to the Presidential Suite sir," said the butler as Phipps stepped inside two double doors.

"This is the last time you'll be using these as this is the way in first time, I'll take you to the entrance and exit you will use during your stay here and we will begin the tour."

A minute or so later they had arrived at another set of double doors,

"Here we are sir, now everything in here, as you would expect is voice activated, but with a difference, it's highly intuitive and emotionally based."

"I see," said Phipps, not seeing at all.

"Ok let's say you would like a swim, you just say pool,"

"This room has a pool?",

"Oh yes sir, there are two, well technically three, the third is a paddling pool for kids really, we are all ready for you, so why don't you try it."

"Try it?"

"Yes sir,"

"Ok pool,"

"Now the green misty light appearing in the flooring is taking you to where you need to go, after you sir."

Phipps followed the soft line from the front doors into a huge reception area. He was amazed, in there were lofty ceilings, sumptuous furniture adorning the room, huge windows to his right with a beautiful view to beyond. Phipps moved away from his path to the pool to check out the view.

"Oh yes sir, the best views in Palomino, and you can control the weather,"

"The weather?"

"Yes sir, try it."

"Erm, let's say thunder,"

"A very nice choice sir."

Clouds instantly gathered outside, and thunderclaps began from afar,

"Well would you believe it," said Phipps.

"Try rain and lightning sir,"

Phipps did, and the system obliged, rain poured against the windows and lightening could be seen.

"fork and sheet" said Phipps

"I beg your pardon sir?" enquired the Butler, apparently shocked by what Phipps had said.

"the lightning, its fork lightening and sheet lightening"

"Indeed sir, would you like to see the pools?"

Following the green flooring guide and several equally appointed rooms later they reached the pools, one inside one outside.

"How many rooms are there in this place?",

"22 sir, well technically 18, four are for your staff."

"Staff?",

"Yes sir, you have a chef, a sous chef and two maids, and me of course, more will arrive according to your needs."

Phipps looked at the larger of the two pools suspended in mid-air beyond the glass and the thundering rain,

"Sun," said Phipps and within seconds the weather had cleared up.

By the pool, neatly folded on one of the many loungers were some towels, swim shorts, robe, and something purple and cold in a glass on a table by their side.

"We took the liberty of scanning you during the shrink, there are many items of clothing which we hope will be to your liking here sir, to make you more comfortable for your stay which you are welcome to take when you leave, will that be all for now sir?"

"Er, yes," said Phipps.

He looked around him in complete amazement at how other people live, he was certainly going to need quite a bit of time to convalesce, a swim whilst he thought about that.

****

Elspeth had been carefully lowered to the base of the wardrobe by her newfound future friends. Attached to the underside of the bed were several hammock type web structures of various sizes for her comfort as she grew to full size to make the next part of her journey. Elspeth saw her own feet padding around the room, occasionally sitting on the bed, and gently bouncing the hidden hammocks below, eventually departing the room for the day and the inevitable arrival of the police. For the first part of her growth, the Commander and crew of the Spider Ship Orb 16 stayed with her as promised. They beamed images of beaches on to the underside of the bed and played meditation music to help her rest, periodically she would roll into a slightly larger hammock until it was time for them to leave.

You awake Elspeth?"

"Yeah I am Ryan,"

"It's time for us to leave now."

Elspeth was about 18 inches long and growing fast, her increased weight gently straining the hammock to the bedroom floor.

"Aww Ryan, I'm going to miss you guys,"

"And the crew are going to miss you,"

"It's a pity I never got to see your face."

All at once a portrait was beamed to the bed underside in front of her,

"That's me," he said, *"And here's the crew,"* seven more portraits appeared.

"Handsome guys,"

"Why thank you mam, not so bad yourself,"

"In my younger days maybe, thanks for babysitting Ryan."

"We aim to please, now good luck and god speed."

Elspeth heard a crackling,

"Orb 16 ready to jump, give me a lock on our verticals, roger that, verticals locked, are we ready to jump, ready to jump commander, go for jump, go for jump."

THAWOO and they were gone.

Elspeth was suddenly overcome by sadness; she was again alone, and a long journey lay ahead. It had been a full twelve hours since she left Jail and another four before her ride home. Now full size, she rolled from underneath the bed, went to the drawers she knew well and found some clothes she thought appropriate for the journey and got dressed. The door opened and Elspeth froze, not daring to look up.

"Oh, I'm sorry mam, I thought you were downstairs,"

"Er no worries, Sally, actually you can help, can you get me a carry case about this big,"

without looking up she waved her arms to imitate the size she required.

"Yes mam," and the maid was gone, Elspeth huffed a sigh of relief.

She rolled back a rug in front of her and lifted the floorboards, she pulled out a large drawstring purse, viewed the contents and then tossed the purse on the bed behind her. In the purse was a fake passport, ID and a large number of credits that looked like casino chips. Cash was largely phased out in the 21st century, making off-market transactions nearly impossible. Instead, everything was online, and very little anonymity was afforded the everyday person. Within 50 years credits were invented, and there were a number of different types available, they had smart chips inside but to all intents and purposes this was good old fashioned cash and Elspeth had a big bag of it. The maid re-entered with the carry case,

"Would you like me to pack something mam?"

"No thank you Sally, but you must not leave this room until you have thoroughly cleaned the top of that wardrobe, it's filthy, heaven only knows what lives up there,"

"Yes mam, right away mam,"

Elspeth smiled to herself as she left the room and crept down the hallway leaving Sally staring at the wardrobe.

****

Phipps sat in a rubber ring in the middle of a suspended pool sipping something purple whilst watching people playing golf somewhere in the distance below him, this really was the life.

"I'm sorry to intrude sir, but there is a call for you, would you like to take it there?"

"Er ok," said Phipps slightly annoyed to be interrupted, slightly curious to know who was calling but also slightly frightened.

"How do I do that?"

"I'll beam it in now sir,"

"I think it might be a private call," said Phipps,

"And so it will be sir, the audio will beam directly into your ears, and just speak normally, I'll give you some privacy," and the butler was gone, if he was even actually there.

Phipps bobbed in the pool for a moment,

"Hello," he said gingerly,

"And how is our patient doing?"

"Oh, it's you,"

"Indeed Mr Phipps, and how are we doing?"

"Ok, under the circumstances, I guess, what do you want?"

"Well first job complete as I hear all is well with the recent operation,"

Phipps made rude signs into the air around him,

"Next, how's the suite?"

"So, you rang to see how my hotel room is, unbelievable, perfectly adequate thank you, anything else?"

"Come, come Mr Phipps, I read the article in Time, have you tried the pool?"

Phipps looked over his left and then right shoulder.

"Seriously Sinclair, what do you want?"

"Ok, ok, to business, you are to ring your daughter, Nicki isn't it? And you are to convince her to come here with Lucy tomorrow, there must be no excuses on their side, they are to drop everything. They need to pack bags for a two week stay, and you would be well to ask Nicki to pack anything small she or Lucy cannot do without".

"Now hold on a minute Sinclair, what's this all about?"

"Well Mr Phipps, I am sure I have no idea, but I am sure you do, and if it is so important that you already lost an organ, albeit one with very little significance which is often removed indiscriminately to avoid complication, then it must be serious, do you not agree?"

Phipps paused for a moment, *"Ok what do I say?"*

"If I am right in assuming Nicki is your daughter then I must also assume you are best placed to know what to say. However, if it were me, I would extol the virtues of your accommodation, as a start, and go from there. Good day Mr Phipps."

There was a sound of a click as the receiver went down the other end.

"Er hello?"

"Yes sir?"

"I need to get hold of my daughter."

Within moments they had connected,

"Dad?",

"Hey Nicki, how are you doing?"

"I'm good, what's going on, you're not seeing Lucy for another few days yet, you never call me at work?"

"I'm sorry honey but this is important, I need you to keep Lucy back from school tomorrow and for the foreseeable future. The same goes for you, you are to pack your bags and come and see me at The Palomino."

"What the little one?"

"Yes,"

"But why Dad? You are really scaring me here?"

"Honey, I've never asked you to do anything crazy before, and I really need you to do this."

"Dad you are really scaring me," a pause, *"Does this have anything to do with a nightmare I told you I had a little while ago?"*

A long pause, *"Promise me you'll come?"*

"I promise."

42
THE GARDENER

Elspeth had made it downstairs, out of the back of the property and to the woods behind the garages. First, she needed a spade from the gardener's shed. The door creaked as she opened it to walk in. She wandered around inside the large space, all sorts of tools hung from or lent against the walls. She grabbed a spade she thought she might be able to use and headed for the spot where she knew the Bayze to be, buried underneath a bench in a clearing in the woods that she and Harold would visit occasionally in the summertime. At the edge of the clearing, she saw Jim, one of the gardeners, tending to the edges of the grass, she had known Jim since she was a child, he kept himself to himself that was for sure, but should she risk an interaction, she knew the rules, but she didn't have time.

"Woo who, hello Jim,"

"Hello mam," said Jim doffing his cap, *"See your going digging, can I help?",*

"Actually yes, you can, but well, it's a secret and I didn't want anyone to know",

"Ah secret is it, best way to keep one of those is not to tell a living soul, my father took a secret to his grave,"

"Oh really?" said Elspeth *"What was that?",*

"I dunno, it was a secret see," Jim winked, Elspeth smiled, she would be ok she thought.

Jim dug up the Bayze and they both walked towards the car garages,

"You go ahead and wait for me there Jim, I'll follow you up," and with that she peeled off towards the treeline.

She reached the edge of the wooded area and saw herself sitting on the patio drinking homemade lemonade as she knew she would, she caught her looking at herself, smiled, waved and retreated back again under cover of the trees, her heart full of joy.

At the garages Jim waited,

"Which one should I take?" she asked,

"Well, there's plenty to choose from, most don't have gas in them right now, but I can organise that,"

"No need," said Elspeth, *"Which one has a full tank of gas and is reliable enough to get me 120 miles or so?"*

"That's easy," said Jim *"Mr Braithwaite, god rest his soul, always used that one as a regular, she's a 1963 E Type Jaguar, nearly 200 years old, although everything, every single nut, bolt, wire, everything has been altered, changed, improved, she's like a brand new car, that's what Mr Braithwaite used to say anyway, god rest his soul."*

"Well, if it was good enough for Harold it will certainly be good enough for me." Sirens could be heard in the distance.

"On the other hand, mam, if I didn't want to attract any attention, I'd take that one, a standard 2154 chevvy people carrier," Elspeth nodded, *"I'll get the keys, back in a jiffy."*

Sure enough, moments later Jim returned, handed Elspeth the keys, and put the package in the case in the boot of the car.

"Now remember what I said Jim," said Elspeth as she tried to hand him a few credits from her stash,

"I've no use for that mam," he replied as he closed her hand over the chips.

The sirens were becoming louder now,

"It's always been a pleasure to serve you, I'll go back to tending those borders now as if nothing had happened and wish you well,"

and with that Jim bent forward, doffed his cap, tapped his nose twice and turned to leave. A nice old fella thought Elspeth.

****

Wolf and the gang were preparing for the meet.

"What's the latest on the warden?"

"He's still there, doctor said because of complications, he can't see anybody right now,"

"And the girl?"

"The mother picked her up from school today, they went straight home, Razor is there now, I'll go take over tonight,"

"Ok good," said Wolf, *"Let's hope his complications ain't fatal, because if we lose the warden, we lose our leverage,"*

"No, the doc said he'd be out tomorrow or the next day latest."

"Ok boys," said Wolf, *"Here's how it's gonna be. You Bull, and Razor will keep an eye on the warden and his family, while me, Zane and Rocky will go to the meet."*

"We're gonna be unarmed in that place boss," said Zane.

"Yeah, I thought of that," said Wolf, *"Tomorrow morning before school, Bull and Razor are going to make a house call and spend some time with the warden's family until the meet is over."*

"Nice one boss," said Zane.

"Ok Rocky, how did you get on with our civilian clothes?"

"Sorted. They're right here boss,"

Rocky tossed a couple of bags, one to Wolf and one to Zane, they both examined the contents of their respective bags.

"Jeez," said Zane,

"This is what civilians wear!" said Rocky defensively, *"Or should we go in wearing our cuts and colours?"*

"Knock it off you two," interrupted Wolf. *"Ok, so we are all set for an 11:00am meet, waiting on a call to find out where in the resort."*

43
THE PREACHER

A man dressed in a suit was visiting each house on the street where Lucy lived with her mother as Razor watched on from the van. He approached each door, rang the bell, porch lights would illuminate, somebody would come to the door, and then close it immediately in front of him, this happened at every house.

"Good evening, sir, I'm from the Church of Religious Discourse. I wonder…" SLAM,

"Good evening, madam, I'm from the Church of…" SLAM,

"Good evening, sir, I'm from the Church of Religious Discourse…" SLAM.

Razor laughed to himself, *"God loves a trier"* he mumbled.

The preacher reached Lucy's house and rang the doorbell,

Nicki answered,

"Wait," he whispered, as Nicki was about to slam the door,

"Your father sent me, now take this leaflet and pretend to read it," Nicki did as she was told,

"There's been a change of plan, you are being watched, don't look up," as Nicki was about to.

"At the bottom of the leaflet there is a number, you can call that in emergencies, we would have phoned but we weren't sure if you were also being listened to,"

"How do I know if you are for real?" said Nicki as matter of fact as she could manage.

"Your father called you today, you are taking lucy to meet him tomorrow, but things are now moving at quite a pace, and we want to get you out of here, what time would you normally take her to school in the morning?"

"8:30am,"

"I see you already have your bags packed," he said as he looked over her shoulder

"Please put them under the stairs after I have gone, someone will take care of those, then lock yourself in for the night." Nicki nodded, she was worried,

"Try not to worry,"

"I don't understand why don't you just arrest them now?",

"It's not the right time, but we do have our own people watching to

keep you safe, I must go soon, a car will be here to pick you up at precisely 7:30am. You must be ready to leave as soon as that car arrives, dress Lucy for school and yourself for work as if it's a normal day, then go straight from the door to the car. One final thing, do you have spare keys?" Nicki nodded, *"Ok good, go and get your purse as if you are handing me some money and give me the keys, it will save us breaking anything when we pick up your luggage."*

Nicki did as she was told.

"Bless you, bless you" he said as he turned and left.

Nicki closed the door and quickly double locked it before putting the cases under the stairs and set about securing the rest of the house.

"Lucy," she yelled up the stairs, *"You are sleeping with Mama tonight."*

44
ASHES

Elspeth had an uneventful drive to The Palomino. The Professor had told her to travel so as not to upset or delay fellow road users in any way and she had managed that, quite well, she thought. She arrived at the vast car park of The Palomino a little over an hour before her planned jump time, left the keys in the glove box and headed for reception. Checking in was a simple affair using her fake ID, but she was supposed to leave her luggage to be sent on afterwards.

"I'm sorry but I'm not leaving this bag with you," she protested, *"In this box,"* she said showing the receptionist her precious parcel *"Are the ashes of my dear departed husband, and they never leave my side, not for a moment,"*

"Well," said the receptionist *"It's quite irregular,"*

"Then you must call the manager," said Elspeth forcefully.

"I'm sure that won't be necessary," said the receptionist *"Let's just*

253

get you through security."

Security, thought Elspeth, this could be difficult. A security guard arrived and led Elspeth to a room just before the shrink portal area.

"Now what appears to be the problem mam?" said the surly guard,

"Well, it's my husband you see, he's in here," she pulled the wrapped parcel from her bag and placed it on the table in front of her, earth still visible.

"It's his ashes, in a lead case, he lives in the garden normally, under our special bench, but I always take him away when I travel."

Nutcase thought the guard, as he lifted the corner of the Bayze.

"That's heavy," he said,

"I know," she replied, *"I was advised by the funeral parlour to get an extra thick lead case as he was to spend most of his time underground, it keeps him safe,"*

"I see…" said the guard, *"…just give me a moment please."*

Elspeth could see the guard talking to his colleague outside through the window, so she began to speak to the box.

"She's a fruitcake, oh Christ, look she's talking to it," said one guard to the other

"What do you think?"

"It's really heavy so there's no doubt its lead, which means there's no point in us x-raying it, and I'm certainly not going to ask her to open

the box up to show us his ashes, what do you want to do?"

"Well, she's no criminal mastermind that's for sure, let's let it slide."

The guard re-entered the room,

"Ok mam, let's get you through,"

"See I told you it would be ok Harold," said Elspeth talking to the box, *"I promised I wouldn't leave your side, this nice man is getting us through,"*

The guard rolled his eyes, *"This way mam,"* and in no time Elspeth was through the shrink portal.

It was a far less glamourous affair than the presidential suite entrance, and a long ride to another reception to pick up the key to room 1537, the closest available room to the landing spot. The professor had been right, the air conditioning system came in through long thin strips just above the skirting boards, and unwrapped, the Bayze fitted snug behind one of the grills in the main living area. Job done she thought, it was just 12 minutes to the jump. She headed for one of the many Palomino Sports Halls to get her ride home. But on arrival at the hall there was a problem, a big one. There was a basketball game in full swing, yet only three minutes until her ride. Two sides were slogging it out and there were at least 30 spectators cheering on. Elspeth walked courtside and tried to get the referees attention, but the game was going at full speed. There was nothing else for it, she walked to the centre of the court, held her arm out for the referee to halt the game. Finally, a whistle was blown, to the jeers of the onlookers. Elspeth turned to address the spectators,

"I am very sorry," she began in a raised voice, *"I am the head of the sports facilities here at The Palomino and we have had reports of a possible gas leak coming from this hall. As a precaution, I am going to ask you all to file out into the area just outside, the check will take no more than three minutes, and all being well, you can continue with your game."*

With that the assembled players and spectators began to leave. Elspeth approached the referee,

"I'm terribly sorry sir, I will run this check, no more than three minutes tops."

There was now only one minute until her ride arrived,

"If you put a timer on your watch, I'll be leaving that way," she waved in the general direction of the other corner of the court, *"If there's a problem, I'll let you know, if not assume, you can play on, again I'm sorry,"*

"No worries," said the referee *"Better safe than sorry,"* he fiddled with his watch and made for the door.

Within moments the ship appeared, and Elspeth clambered in to be greeted by Millie in the cockpit,

"GO!" she shouted and THAWOOO, and they were gone.

****

Nicki had not slept a wink, she decided to get up early, get ready and busy herself until it was time to wake Lucy.

"Come on honey, today's the day we are going to see Gramps,"

"Yeah,"

"I need you to get your school uniform on,"

"But I thought I was missing school to see Gramps?",

"Well yes, you will be seeing Gramps, but I need you to get your school uniform on,"

"But if I'm not going…",

"Stop," Nicki interrupted *"If you want to see Gramps you put your school uniform on now, understood?"*

"Yes Mummy."

Outside in the van, Bull was waiting for Razor to arrive,

"Jeez this place stinks," he said as he opened the door and handed Bull a coffee and a sandwich.

"Any news Bull?"

"Nothing overnight, lights out about midnight, a bum has appeared, he's sitting on the bench up there drinking hooch."

"Ok, so we'll have breakfast and then pay them a visit. Wolf wants us to babysit until the meeting's over, he reckons about lunchtime, and he says if they give us any trouble, we're to rough 'em up some,"

"Well yes sir," said Bull gleefully.

The tramp got up and began to stagger towards them, swigging from a bottle of bourbon, stumbling into the road and approaching the front of the van.

"Get your greasy ass out of here," shouted Razor through the windscreen as he gestured for him to get out of the road.

At that moment a car pulled up outside Nicki's house, the door opened, and Nicki and Lucy appeared making their way to the car,

"look sharp, we have movement," said Bull,

"Jeez," said Razor, and in the blink of an eye Nicki and Lucy were in the car and it pulled away.

"Run that bum over if you have to but don't lose that car," Bull fired the engine into life, the tramp moved to one side, and they were in pursuit.

The tramp lifted a radio from inside his clothing,

"We have the package, but we have a tail."

"Roger that Rogue One, go get yourself cleaned up, then pick up the luggage,"

"Roger that control, Rogue One out."

In the van Razor flipped open his phone,

"Boss we've got a problem, yeah we're tailing them now, no we won't lose them,"

Razor flipped the phone shut,

"The boss is pissed,"

"No shit, where do you think they are going? It ain't school, that's for sure?"

****

Some 30 minutes later the car pulled up outside The

Columbia University Medical Centre.

Doctor Sinclair met the two visitors at reception,

"You must be Nicki and you, little one, must be the lovely Lucy? Gramps has a got a treat in store for you young lady, now if you'd like to follow me,"

"But why are we here?" said Nicki,

"It's a precaution, you are just passing through, there's a car out the back to take you to your final destination."

****

"Yup, they're at the hospital," said Bull,

"Came to see the warden, ok boss, we'll let you know." A pause *"Boss wants us to find out what's going on and then sit tight here until they leave so I'm gonna see my buddy the doctor."*

With that, Bull left the van and made for the hospital reception.

Doctor Sinclair was waiting for him,

"Well, our patient is popular today, and how are you, Mr?"

"How's he doing?" Bull interrupted,

"Well, we think he'll be fine, his daughter and granddaughter are seeing him now," said the doctor.

"I wanna see him," said Bull,

"Immediate family only, I'm afraid, are you immediate family?"

"I wanna see him," Bull insisted.

"I'm afraid that won't be possible, and we don't want any trouble here, we don't want to have to call the police Mr, actually what is your name sir?"

"I'm gonna come check on him again in a hour," and with that Bull span on his heels and left.

45
HOMECOMING

"Am I pleased to see you!" said Millie as she handed Elspeth a prison uniform,

"How did it go? The mission was 16 hours, and I'm sure I'll never get used to it but you've only been gone from here for no more than 20 minutes."

"Eventful to say the least," said Elspeth. *"I'm going to need to see Freddie as soon as I'm changed",*

"Yeah, there's a debrief in the canteen in five minutes,"

"Great let' go, I'll leave my other clothes in the ship," and with that the two headed for the canteen.

"So how was it Elspeth?" said Jack,

"Eventful," repeated Elspeth, *"I had to clear the sports hall,"*

"Ok," said Freddie *"That's not shown up as a problem, but your disappearance from the resort has. We need to make a plan for you to go straight back and find a way to check out, I anticipated this, and Jack has been in touch with Jimmy. Apparently check out was quite crude when they first opened the resort so it should be a quick fix, but you'll have to show up sorry."*

"No worries," said Elspeth, *"The problem is the drop zone was obviously being used back then, how are we going to get around that?"*

"We'll take you back to when you first cleared the hall, Millie will fit a time lapse camera and she'll retrieve it at 1:00am, we have to assume it will be empty then, we'll review the footage and hopefully, we'll have a slot for you just after the game has finished, if you are happy to be lifted we'll see you on the time lapse and come scoop you up,"

"That's genius Freddie," said Elspeth, *"When do I go?"*

"Now," said Freddie *"We can't risk the tremor making its way back to us here, no time like the present, Millie will brief you,"* and with that the two ladies made their way back to the craft.

"So," began Millie, *"You'll head straight to reception, tell them something about having to leave in an emergency. They will give you a form that you will take to the exit area, hand in the form, make sure people around you see that you are there, be loud,"*

"No problem for me,"

"There will be about 100 people leaving at that time so mingle in the crowd, you'll see a staff only door to the left, you are to go through that, the only other door in that room will lead you to a corridor, and then another door back into the public areas, then back to the hall."

Both women strapped in, dials turned and checked,

THAWOO, they were in the hall. Elspeth still dressing left for her mission, Millie jumped out to fit the time lapse camera, and jumped back in again. THAWOO, it was 1:00am in the same place, Millie retrieved the camera, rewound, found Elspeth on the time lapse, turned the dials again and THAWOO. Elspeth jumped back in, 22 minutes after she had left but for Millie the whole mission had been completed in less than a minute.

"Hey honey," said Elspeth as she clambered in,

"Hey Elspeth, everything ok?"

"I think so," said Elspeth,

"Ok, tomorrow on this timeline the resort will receive an email from you saying how sorry you were to leave and how much you are looking forward to returning, let's go see if the patch worked."

THAWOOO and they were back in the east wing of Green River 5.

****

Nicki and Lucy had arrived at The Presidential Suite, the only difference on their journey in was there were two seats at the shrink portal, one large, one small, and the butler greeted them on arrival.

"Well good afternoon, madam, you must be Nicki, and you, young lady must be Lucy," Lucy clung to her mother's leg smiling.

"This is the last time you will use this entrance; I'll take you to the doors you'll be using during your stay and then straight to see your Grandpa young lady."

The butler took the two of them to the standard doors and then onto one of the vast living areas, a wall of glass to the right, sun streaming in. There standing in front of them was Phipps, he was wearing a sky-blue cashmere tracksuit, white tee shirt, baseball cap set at a jaunty angle and white sliders on his feet. Apart from the absence of any gold he looked like a 21st Century rap artist.

"Dad," enquired Nicki,

"Gramps!" shouted Lucy as she ran to embrace him.

"Hey girls, am I glad to see you."

"Now then," said the butler, *"Is anyone hungry, we do a lovely breakfast?"* Nicki nodded.

"And young Lucy, you look like you might really love chocolate waffles, why don't you come and help me make them? I think Mummy and Grampa have got some catching up to do."

"It's Gramps, not Grandpa," said Lucy,

"Oh well I will remember that," said the butler as he took Lucy's hand and led her away.

"Jeez Dad, what the hell have you got us mixed up in here, I didn't get a wink last night. Some criminals have been watching the house, and some guy turned up last night to give me a message. What's going on?"

"Gosh," said Phipps, *"Where do I start?"*

"Try the beginning," said Nicki abruptly,

"Well, let's start with the nightmare," said Phipps sombrely, *"You*

264

see it wasn't a nightmare, it was a reality, an old reality." Nicki held her head in her hands and began to sob,

"I didn't have a choice really as I saw it," said Phipps comforting his daughter, *"It all started with a conversation with some people I look after in one of the prisons,"*

"You mean some criminals?" Phipps nodded,

"They helped bring Lucy back you see, and they are actually good people. I helped them get something and in return they helped us get Lucy back."

Phipps went on to explain how he had retrieved the Bayze and delivered it to the prison.

"But how come, if your friends are such good people as you put it, I've had a couple of thugs outside my house, and I've had to visit a hospital only to leave through the back door. I'm also pretty certain I've seen that van outside the school, one of the parents mentioned it a couple of days back, how come Dad?"

"Well Nicki," Phipps began *"You know that break out recently, Backman and his gang, it was all over the news?"*

"Don't tell me you had something to do with that?",

"No, no, I didn't, nothing at all, it was completely unrelated. But they found out that I helped the others, and they have been putting the pressure on me."

"Oh, jeez dad, what are we going to do, and why are you here?"

"I am here because my friends are trying to help us, all three of us, it's in their interest to get a good outcome as much as it's in ours. As I see

it, we have two options, option one, we go to the authorities, I go to jail and you lose Lucy forever, and option two, we sit tight and let this thing play out. I'm for option two, I risked everything to get her back, and I don't want to lose her again."

Lucy came bounding into the room in a swimsuit, a rubber ring around her waist, and her face covered in chocolate,

"Gramps, there's a giant unicorn in my room, rainbows on the wall, and cartoons on the ceiling! Where's the pool? I'm going swimming, come on Mummy."

Lucy had lifted the mood, a timely reminder, if Nicki needed it, about why her father had gone to desperate lengths. The three of them went outside and Phipps and his daughter watched on as Lucy splashed around in her very own pool.

46
FIRST CONTACT

Wolf snapped his phone shut,

"Ok we're all ready to go here, the boys are keeping an eye on the hospital, we should get ourselves ready to saddle up".

"What about the fact that we don't have the women in custody?", said Zane,

"I'm not bothered, Palmer knows I can get to the warden and his family anytime I want, it don't change a thing, now let's get down there early. We'll all check in separate, and once we're inside, we'll meet up at the big bar, it's always busy apparently, and remember, we've gotta blend in, we're just three friends taking a well-earned break."

The three men gathered themselves and left their hideout, each taking separate pre-booked taxis from a corner down the street. Wolf arrived first, using his fake ID, check in was simple and before too long he was in his room. Rocky followed and then Zane, it was 9:30am. The men met in the big bar at 10:00am, exactly one hour before the meet.

"What's the plan Wolf?" said Rocky,

"The plan Rocky, is we meet up, we get the machine, we leave."

"Good morning gentlemen, can I help you?" said the waitress,

"Three beers please," said Zane,

"Ah, breakfast of champions," said the waitress, *"Coming right up."*

The phone rang, *"Palmer, I hope you are not calling me to tell me there's a problem?"* Wolf listened intently, *"Well that's not my problem. Ok, ok, you come to me, we're in the big bar, see you here,"* he snapped the phone shut.

"Palmer says he's coming but he doesn't have the machine, not yet."

****

Jack, Millie, Elspeth and Freddie were getting ready for the jump and Jack's meeting with Wolf and the gang.

"Don't you think it's a risk to turn up empty handed Jack?" said Freddie,

"No," said Jack, *"They are committed now, even if they left the resort, it will be 12 hours until they are full size, they have to wait to hear what I have to say,"*

"But are you delaying this because you don't want to give them the Bayze? Because if you are, we have a solution?" said the professor,

"A solution?" said Jack and Millie in unison,

"Why didn't you tell us?" said Millie.

"I can't say more now but whatever happens with this lot I promise we will still have a Bayze," said the professor, *"You'll just have to trust us for now,"*

"Us?" said Millie,

"Yes," said Elspeth *"Us."* Millie and Jack eyed the others in disbelief,

"Ok," said the professor, *"You go have your meeting Jack, but arrange that we will do the handover at 1:00pm. We'll get everything ready here for our departure as planned, to be honest we could do with an extra couple of hours anyway."*

****

After the jump with Millie, Jack left The Palomino sports hall and went straight to the big bar. He sat in front of Wolf,

"Wolf," nodded Jack,

"Palmer, this better be good,"

"We've had an impromptu shakedown and roll call, we'll be good to go in a couple of hours,"

"How come you managed to get here, won't you be missed? And doesn't that mean the machine is here?"

Jack looked at his watch, *"I've got precisely eight minutes before I am missed, and if I am it won't be good for any of us, and that includes you, now do you want to hear what I have to say or not, we don't have much time?"*

269

"Go ahead," said Wolf,

"Well we know you're going to hit The Union Bank," Wolf shifted uncomfortably in his chair.

"It's a good target, they hold all the city's credits and they've been activated, they are untraceable but, your plan won't work. On the other hand, my plan will,"

"What do you mean your plan?"

"We've been watching you, we've run the numbers, it won't work, our plan is better, and it will work for you, but I have conditions."

"What do you mean watching us?" said Wolf angrily,

"We've got eyes on you, we want to make sure you do what you say you are going to do. You sing a lot of Elvis by the way," said Jack.

Wolf looked very uncomfortable now,

"You've got a nerve coming here, making demands," he was losing it now,

"They are not demands," said Jack calmly, *"They are conditions, and without your agreement, we don't have a deal, and I walk."*

There was a long pause as the two men held each other's gaze, until finally Wolf regained his cool.

"Talk," he said finally,

"We do this, you get the machine, you leave Phipps and his family alone, not just for now but for good," said Jack

"Is that it?" said Wolf,

270

"One more thing, and this is advice, not a condition, you've no experience in jumping, if you are not very careful, you'll get caught and quickly. Do this job and then learn everything you can about what you have, it's a very powerful thing, I was trained by the military, and I got caught, you've been warned."

"So, what's the plan?" said Wolf,

"Do we have an agreement?" said Jack, and Wolf nodded.

"Ok," began Jack, *"Here's what you need to do,"*

Jack spent the next few minutes explaining his version of the plan, before heading back to Millie, and both returned back to the east wing.

****

Phipps sat with his daughter watching Lucy splashing about in the paddling pool.

"So, what do you think Nicki?"

"I think you've been very brave Dad; I agree we don't want things to go back to the way that they were, but I am worried about the mess we are in right now,"

"I know," said Phipps, *"It's far from ideal, but I've come to learn that these time travellers are not bad people, ok they broke the law, but really they are just adventurers, they are really smart too, you know there are three top scientists amongst their number."*

Nicki thought for a moment, *"Ok, I'll help in whatever way I can."*

"Excuse me sir?" said the butler, *"There's a telephone call for you,"*

271

"Pipe it through," said Phipps over his shoulder.

"Hello?"

"And how's my favourite patient?"

"Good morning Sinclair, I'm well thank you, I have visitors so I can't spend long talking to you, what do you want?"

"Ah yes, Nicki and Lucy, lovely I'm sure they are enjoying the facilities?"

"Yes thank you, now what do you want?" said Phipps abruptly,

"You are to head down to the big bar immediately, Backman is there with two other gang members," Phipps heart sunk, *"You are to sit down in the booth next to theirs, it will be free when you arrive, you are to make sure you are not seen,"*

"What should I do?" said Phipps quizzically.

"Nothing, you are just to sit tight for as long as you can without being seen, something about CCTV footage, sit for not less than 10 minutes apparently, that's it, good luck, have a nice day," there was a click as the receiver went down.

Phipps nervously prepared for his mission.

****

Downstairs, Wolf, Zane and Rocky were sat drinking beer when a phone rang,

"Hey Bull, what's up?" Wolf listened intently for a few moments, *"How the hell did they get past you?"* another pause, *"Ok, so get to the school and wait."* Wolf snapped the phone

shut.

"What's up boss?" said Rocky,

"The warden has been released, he's convalescing apparently, Doc doesn't know where,"

"And the women?"

"He thinks the girl has gone to school as she had her uniform on this morning, they left through a different exit, stupid idiot, you think he would have checked all of that at the start."

The three men sat in silence. Phipps saw the men from a distance as he approached, he was careful to make a big circle around the table before approaching, and as he did two people got up from the booth next to theirs, Phipps sat down, pulled a news tablet from a bag he was carrying and pretended to read. The three men were still not talking.

"Good morning, sir," said the waitress as she glided up to Phipps' booth, *"And what can I get for you?"*

"Coffee please, and two eggs over easy," Phipps thought food might be something of a distraction from his current position.

"Very good sir," she moved to Wolf's booth, *"And gentlemen, one more round?"* Zane nodded, the men sat in silence, Phipps waited, time moved slowly.

****

Back in the east wing the four travellers stood in a huddle once more,

"So Jimmy…" began Jack,

"The serial killer," interjected Millie,

"So Jimmy," said Jack starting again, *"has agreed to stand in with the gang, it's a risk but he's prepared to take it."*

"And how are we going to do the switch?" said the professor,

"I've thought about that Freddie, leave it to me,"

"Ok, if you are sure, now how are we getting on with everything else?"

"The safe house is ready," said Millie *"I've run the time lapse camera, across the entirety of our stay and everything looks good, the only change will be our presence there when the time comes,"*

"Good job Millie," said Jack, *"How are we doing with the cameras here Freddie?"*

"All set, I estimate we'll have a good four hours before Danny's radio in to control. I've been recording him, and those messages are largely not interactive so I'm working on an automatic report from him, and if they buy it, we'll have 8 hours, but best to assume four,"

"That's great work Freddie, so that just leaves Danny," everyone looked at Millie.

"Well," said Millie, *"I can distract him, we can overpower him and tie him up, but what if there were another way, what if he was to come with us?"*

"What?" said Jack *"You can't be serious,"*

"Well," said Millie, *"I would like to give him the choice, he's been good to me, well, all of us really, in one way or another. I think he's*

one of the good guys and I'd like to give him the choice."

"I can't say I like it Millie," said the professor, *"But I understand why you are saying this"*

"I disagree strongly," said Jack, *"This move could end up jeopardising everything",*

"I'm voting with Millie," said Elspeth, *"It is not without its risks, but Millie knows Danny the best, Danny will have no future in the system once they discover what has happened here, he should be given the choice, but no emotion Millie. We follow the plan and when we are leaving, we ask the question once, we read his answer and we act accordingly, I'll come with you when the time comes, agreed?"*

"Agreed," said Millie,

"So that's settled," said the professor,

"I don't like it one bit," said Jack,

"Well, you've been outvoted," said Elspeth *"Now let's move on, I'll get some tea,"*

"I'll come with you," said Millie, as they both got up to go to the tea machine.

"Jack is acting real weird," whispered Millie, *"He was watching those videos again, I mean how can you do that again and again,"*

"Well," began Elspeth, *"He's having to speak to his brother quite a bit at the moment, it's got to be difficult for him, best we concentrate on the job in hand. Now after I've had my tea, I need to pay Mr Phipps a visit in person, will you take me? I'll need 25 minutes."*

"Roger that," said Millie.

47
CCTV

Wolf, Zane and Rocky had been sitting in silence, sipping their beers when the phone rang,

"Bull?" said Wolf.

Phipps sat eating his eggs, listening in,

"Ok, well you've no choice but to go back to base, go back to their house this evening when the mother finishes work,"

Phipps suspected this conversation was about Nicki and Lucy and he was right.

"One last thing Bull, you need to know I'm not happy, this has been a poor job, now make sure you make this right," and with that he snapped the phone shut.

"Bull and Razor have been moved on from the school, a complaint from one of the parents so they're headed back to base, they'll pay our friends a visit tonight."

Phipps sat frozen to his seat, thank goodness Nicki and Lucy were with him, he drew some comfort from the fact that they had no idea about this which meant they probably had no idea about him. On the next pass by the waitress, he asked for the check and headed back to his room, he knew he had been there for at least 20 minutes although it had seemed far, far longer. The whole episode was being watched by Jimmy Palmer who was sat in an office somewhere in the resort, looking at the monitors in front of him. He stopped the record button and pulled a flash drive from the computer beside him, put it in his pocket, and left the room. Elspeth had left the Palomino sports hall with the carry bag over her shoulder, she saw the big bar in the distance and made her way around the side of the vast indoor space, with shops of all types, the sort you would find in any hotel. Walking towards her was Jimmy Palmer, and as they passed each other he palmed her two things, a flash drive, and a room key. They continued without stopping in opposite directions.

Elspeth reached her room and opened her hand to reveal the flash drive, a CCTV recording of Phipps sitting in the booth next to the three criminals and a key to the door of room 1537. This time, she was also armed with a screwdriver, and she made light work of the grill. The Bayze was just where she had left it six years earlier, and next to it, the big bag of credits. She placed both in her large carry bag. Next stop was the presidential suite.

"You have a visitor," said the butler, just as Phipps had sat down after his adventure at the big bar,

"Who is it?" said Phipps,

"A Mrs Braithwaite, she says you are expecting her,"

No, I wasn't thought Phipps, *"Oh yes,"* he said, *"Please send her in."*

A few moments later Elspeth entered the large reception room where Phipps sat while Nicki and Lucy were outside playing in the paddling pool. Elspeth was impressed with the suite, she had stayed in the world's best hotels but this, this was as good as she had seen, although, as you would expect from a woman of her breeding, she didn't give it away in her manner.

"Would you mind ensuring miss Lucy is entertained whilst I speak to Mr Phipps and his daughter?" the butler looked at Phipps and he nodded,

"Very good madam," he said and off he went towards the pools.

Some moments later Nicki entered the room, walked towards Elspeth, and held out her hand,

"I'm Nicki Phipps, I'm very pleased to meet you",

"Elspeth Braithwaite, likewise, please take a seat, I thought it time for the three of us to have a chat, I don't have long before I'm missed,"

Elspeth looked at Phipps and winked, Phipps looked at his feet.

"I'll be as quick as I can," began Elspeth, *"We were in a position, with the resources at our disposal, to help you and your family to change a most unfortunate event for the better,"*

"I've given Nicki the details," said Phipps,

"Good, then you will also know that part one of the plan has worked without any time tremor ramifications, so in that sense we have a new reality, you will also know we now have a rather nasty problem to deal with,"

"Yes," said Nicki, *"Dad has told me about the gang, do they know about the new reality?"*

"No," said Elspeth, *"They have no way of joining those dots, but it is a big problem nevertheless, we believe we have a solution, and your father will be a part of that solution, but first thing's first, I'll tell you about that in a moment."*

"Go on," said Phipps,

"Even if we solve this problem in the short term, the man we are dealing with is also very resourceful, the three of you will never be safe if you stay here,"

"What in the hotel?" said Nicki,

"No," said Elspeth, *"In the lives you currently have, you will have to start again".*

"You mean leave the city?" said Nicki,

"No," said Elspeth, *"You must leave the country,"* silence fell over the room.

"Where will we go?" said Nicki finally,

"Well, that's up to you, here's a list of suggestions,"

Elspeth pulled some paper from her pocket with a list of

glamourous locations,

"All have excellent schools, you'll be given new identities and you will be very well looked after, you will not have to work again, unless you want to, of course."

"There's no other option here?" questioned Phipps.

"No," said Elspeth *"There is no other way if you want things to stay as they are, that is to have Lucy in your lives,"*

"Can't you just go back to the past and make sure the gang didn't escape?" said Nicki,

"No," said Elspeth, *"The event has had so much coverage, the time tremors would become earthquakes, it's just not possible, to my mind there is no other way."*

"So, what's next?" said Phipps,

"Take a look at the list, you have a little time to decide about that, we will take care of the rest, Mr Phipps, you are to wait precisely one hour 35 minutes and then call the police, here's your script,"

Elspeth pulled another piece of paper from her pocket and handed it to Phipps.

"Take the time now to learn that back to front, that is exactly the conversation you heard the gang having when you sat down, the time clock has been set on the CCTV to show that you will actually be sitting down in just over an hour, so it is imperative you make the call at exactly the time I have said, you can do it from here, is that clear?"

"Yes, I think so," said Phipps,

"You must know so," said Elspeth staring at Phipps.

"*Understood,*" he said,

"*And what about this new life?*" said Nicki, "*New identities?*",

"*Yes,*" said Elspeth, "*You will all have new names, although we'll leave Lucy's first name as it is, to try to mitigate as much confusion for her as we can,*",

"*You've thought of everything,*" said Nicki,

"*We hope so,*" said Elspeth, "*Take this,*" she handed the big bag of credits to Nicki,

"*Those are cross border credits so you can legally carry them into other countries without difficulty, there is enough there to get you started and we'll have you set up the other end,*"

Nicki peered in the bag.

"*Wow,*" she said, "*Thank you,*"

"*Not at all,*" said Elspeth.

Lucy ran into the room dripping wet from the pool.

"*Gramps come and watch me jump in,*"

Elspeth looked at Lucy with loving eyes, this had all been worth it, she thought.

"*Come say hi to auntie Elspeth,*" said Nicki,

"*Hello young lady,*" said Elspeth,

"*Hello auntie, want to watch me jump in?*"

"*I would like that very much,*" said Elspeth as she took Lucy's hand to be led to one of the pools.

Phipps looked at his daughter,

"We have no choice here Nicki," he said, *"We've no other family, it's always just been the three of us."*

"And I hate my boss," said Nicki, they both laughed,

"I worry about Lucy though," said Phipps,

"There's no need," said Nicki, *"She'll make new friends, it will be a great adventure for her,"*

"Ok so it's settled," said Phipps, *"Let's have a look at that list."*

****

Wolf and the others were on their third beer when the phone rang again.

"Palmer, go ahead."

Wolf listened intently for a few minutes before snapping the phone shut.

"What's up boss?" said Rocky,

"Palmer says we are on for 1:00pm, we are meeting in a room, number 1537. Someone's going to bring a key, we have to sit tight here in the meantime. Zane, go to one of those shops over there, buy three rucksacks, we need food and drink, get enough for a day."

At that moment Jimmy walked past the table, and dropped a key without stopping,

"Hey Palmer," shouted Wolf, but Jimmy kept walking.

Wolf got up to follow, but Jimmy was around the corner of the bar and disappeared into a crowd gathered for a celebration of some kind.

Wolf returned to the table and picked up the key card,

"This guy is really getting on my nerves," he said,

"Hey boss, it looks like we are definitely on, he wouldn't be going to this much trouble if he was going to give us to the feds,"

Wolf sat back down,

"Just go get what I said," and with that Zane went shopping.

Wolf and Rocky sat in silence again,

"Good afternoon gentlemen," said the waitress, *"How are we doing?"*

"Three club sandwiches and three more beers," said Wolf without looking up.

"Right you are sir," said the waitress as she scribbled on a pad, before walking off.

"What I don't get…" started Wolf, *"Is why this guy is so important to them?"*

"What do you mean boss?" said Rocky,

"Well if it was me, I'd burn the warden, I mean they are going to give us a machine, just to save his skin, he must know something, something they don't want us to know, those machines are worth a fortune on the black market, and they are really hard to get hold of too, and yet he's giving it to us, something doesn't add up." Wolf thought for a

moment, *"We'll take Palmer with us on the job, we'll make it a condition,"*

"You think he'll agree?" said Rocky,

"I think he has to, this warden is real important and I don't know why, but even if we don't have him now, we can get to him, real easy, we'll use that as leverage." Rocky smiled. *"Take this key, go find the room, take a look around and then get back here,"* and with that Rocky got up to leave.

Wolf sat alone, thinking, it was 12:10pm and after 10 minutes Rocky returned.

"It's not far from here boss, it's on this level, that way," he pointed in the general direction of the room. *"It's a standard suite, living area and two bedrooms, I gave it a good shakedown, nothing,"*

"Ok, thanks," said Wolf as Zane re-joined the group, carrying three rucksacks with food and drink in them.

Soon after the beers and clubs arrived, it's not long now thought Wolf.

"Go get one more rucksack and food for another person."

****

The east wing of Green River 5 was a hive of activity as the inmates prepared for their departure, everyone had been briefed and told to behave normally but the atmosphere was one of great excitement. Danny caught up with Millie,

"Everyone seems a bit excited today Millie, what's going on?"

"There's a game on later," said Millie, *"I think someone is running*

a book, it's of no interest to me though."

If it was of no interest to Millie, it would be of no interest to Danny, she thought, and she was right, there was no game and she didn't want Danny to be discovering that back at his desk.

"I'm looking forward to watching that new series starting on Friday on channel ZED though, it's a drama, I can't remember the name," she said, Danny made a mental note,

"I better get on," he said,

"I wanted to talk to you privately." said Millie.

"I'll come and see you in a bit if that's ok?"

"Sure," said Danny as he walked away, he always looked forward to seeing Millie.

Millie made her way to pick up Elspeth from The Palomino and Jack and the professor sat together making last minute plans.

"Ok," Jack began, *"I'll meet them in the room and go through the machine,"*

"I'm coming with you," said the professor,

"Well that's not part of the plan Freddie",

"Plans change Jack, you need some back up there,"

"Are you worried I won't hand over the Bayze Freddie?" said Jack,

"Not at all," said Freddie, but this was a lie. *"I just think you*

need someone else in there with you, I can give them some technical jargon to make sure they treat what they have with some sort of respect,"

Jack thought for a moment,

"It can't hurt I suppose, unless they decide they want to take you with them and then we really are scuppered,"

"No, they'll want to take you and anyway, we'll insist upon it."

Elspeth and Millie joined them, Elspeth threw the flash drive at the professor,

"CCTV from Jimmy," she said,

"Did you speak to him?" said Jack quickly,

"No, just a hand over," said Elspeth,

"Check you are happy with the footage Freddie, I've not seen it, also that the timecode on the recording meets our needs,"

"Roger that," said the professor.

"And the other thing?"

"In a bag in the back of the ship,"

The professor left to review the recording and test the Bayze that Elspeth had brought back.

"The other thing?" asked Millie,

"All will be revealed, you know how Freddie is about these sorts of things and he's always right,"

"Fair enough," said Millie. *"How did it go with Phipps?"*

"If all goes to plan, he is due to call the cops at the same time the meeting happens in the room, how are you doing Jack?"

"I'm ok, just want to get this thing over so we can get our people out,"

"Amen to that," said Elspeth.

The professor re-joined the group,

"The footage is good, the timeline correct, and the new Bayze is in working order,"

"New Bayze?" said Jack,

"Yup," said Elspeth, *"You didn't think we were going to let them have the only toy in town did you honey?"*

"I'm impressed," said Jack.

"Way to go," said Millie, *"Did this have anything to do with your mission to the doctors?",*

"Now, now people, the how and why are not important here, you know that; the fact is we have a second machine,"

Jack clapped his hands, Millie and the professor joined in, and Elspeth took a bow.

48
THE MEET

Wolf decided they should get to the meeting place early, so they arrived at the room at 12:45pm, carried out a thorough sweep of the two bedrooms in 1537, before settling in the main living area to await Jack's arrival. Time slowed down once more. Finally, at the stroke of 1:00pm precisely, an almost imperceivable THAWOO, and Jack entered the living area from one of the bedrooms, followed by the professor.

"Good afternoon gentlemen."

Wolf and the others looked at Jack opened mouthed; they had expected a knock at the door.

"Well, that's some kind of entrance," said Wolf, *"Let's get down to business."*

Jack and the professor moved to sit down on one of the

sofas in the living area, Rocky got up and sat opposite them next to Wolf and Zane. Jack placed the Bayze on the table.

"Gentlemen, this is Freddie, my associate, he knows everything there is to know about travel,"

Jack looked at his watch,

"We have precisely 14 minutes to go through the operation of this machine, go through the plan again, and send you on your way."

Wolf interrupted, *"Actually, I wanted to mention one of our conditions,"*

Jack looked up from the Bayze,

"You're coming with us,"

"That wasn't in the plan," said Jack,

"Let's just call it insurance," smirked Wolf, *"Or maybe we'll take him,"* he said pointing at the professor.

"If anybody goes, it's going to be me," said Jack.

"Good," said Wolf, *"So it's settled, now let's go through the plan and then you can show me how this thing works."*

"Right," said Jack, as he pulled some paper from his pocket,

"The first set of numbers represent longitude and latitude, that is where you want to go, and that set there takes you to inside the safe of The Union Bank, ok?"

"Ok, where do we get those from?" said Wolf, and the professor interjected,

"These numbers have been used for many hundreds of years, to pinpoint locations around the globe, like imaginary lines, when you put two numbers together you get a cross, like a target, longitude goes from north to south and latitude from east to west,"

"I get it," said Wolf, *"Like GPS?"*

"Yes, exactly," said the professor,

"And what's the other one?" said Rocky,

"That's the time, the when," said the professor, *"Look, the time now is 1:05pm on the 22nd August 2162, right?"*

"Right…"

"Look, so the dial reads 002162.08.22.13.05.00.00,"

the last four digits seconds and tenths of seconds carried on spinning.

"So," the professor continued, *"the first is the where, the second is the when."*

The three men sat in silence, although this was simple stuff, they had not seen anything like it before, and Wolf was concerned.

"Don't worry," said Jack, *"I said I would come with you, but it is important you understand how it works. As much as I like you guys,"* he said sarcastically, *"I won't be hanging around after the job is done."*

Wolf smiled, *"So what next?"*

"We jump," said Jack, *"But if I'm coming with you, I'll need to*

change, I won't get far in this prison uniform, give me five minutes, I'll leave Freddie and the machine with you,"

"Make it quick," said Wolf.

Jack left the room, this time by the front door.

"Ok gentlemen," said the professor, *"We are going to set the time to 12 hours before now, you will arrive in the safe and then there's a long wait I'm afraid, you must wait a full 14 hours before you leave, 12 hours to become fully grown and a further two hours to get the job done. You must be fully grown and able to work, the second set of numbers on your piece of paper are the coordinates of your hideout. You must load everything you wish to take from the bank in the centre of the safe, there is plenty of room, and then when the time comes, hit this jump button here and you will be back at your hideout, you will jump back to this timeline,"* the professor flicked the boomerang switch, *"And the coordinates are locked."*

"Woohoo," shouted Rocky, *"I love it,"*

"Pipe down Rocky," said Wolf.

"And that's it," said the professor, *"Shall we synchronize our watches in preparation for Jack?"*

Jack met Jimmy in the corridor, and they went into the room next door,

"Are you ready to do this?"

"Yes, I'm ready, I will keep my mouth shut, funny enough when I dropped the key at the table, they thought it was you, so fingers crossed."

Jimmy entered room 1537 ready to take a journey with three

murdering criminals. It was 1:13pm and he was nervous,

"Palmer lets go,"

within minutes the four men stood together, the professor watching on from a distance. THAWOO and they were gone.

Moments later Jack re-entered the room, tossed the professor some civilian clothes,

"Shall we go home?" he said, the professor nodded, they left the room.

Jack turned and kicked the door in,

"They broke into the room," he said to the professor, and they walked down the corridor to get their ride home.

49
THE CALL

At precisely 1:00pm, Phipps from the comfort of his luxurious surroundings, made the call,

"New York Police Department, Inspector Peterson please,"

"Peterson here,"

"I want to report a serious crime."

Phipps went on to explain about his recent operation, his convalescence, and his chance encounter at the big bar where he overheard the three criminals discussing the Union Bank Job, a time machine, he had even overheard something about a hideout in a named warehouse in a run-down part of town. He explained about the kidnapping of the resort manager, in effect he had overheard the whole plan. An incident room was set up, Phipps was beamed in through video link, every aspect of what he had heard was turned over again and again, there was no point going to the safe, the criminals would not be there anymore as the crime had already taken place, their best chance was to catch them when they returned to the safehouse in real time, they had two hours at best. Nobody doubted Phipps story, he was an upstanding member of the community, in an important job in the prison system, all focus moved to the hideout. If there was any doubt whatsoever about Phipps story, it dissipated when Bull and Razor were found there, a gun battle ensued, they weren't going quietly. An officer was wounded, and both felons were killed. The police cordoned off the area, there was no chance of escape, a plan was hatched to use gas, but the warehouse area was vast so they quickly ditched that plan as they couldn't make the whole thing airtight. Extra care was taken at every step, after all they had a hostage.

****

Twelve hours or so before Phipps had even made the call, the gang arrived in the huge safe of The Union Bank and prepared for a long wait, it was 1:15am on Saturday morning, and by around 3:00pm they would be out.

"Palmer," said Wolf, *"This shit is crazy, I can't get my head around the fact that we are doing this 12 hours before we even left to do it,"*

"I know!" said Jimmy, *"It really does twist your noodle, now I'm going to get some rest, we've a long wait ahead of us,"* and with that he laid down and pulled a rucksack under his head.

The others sat cross legged in a circle, went through their individual bags to find food and drink, like kids on a school outing who start eating as soon as they get on the bus. After six hours the inevitable back aches began, Wolf knew this feeling from when he grew in his cell in preparation for his fight with the previous boss of Green River 8. A few more hours and they were able to begin work, a few more and they were almost ready to leave. Jimmy helped but avoided conversation at all costs. Finally,

"Palmer, how come the extra two hours?"

Jimmy didn't know what to say, he thought for a moment,

"Well, we looked at this and it was the optimum amount of time," it sounded good he thought,

"I see," said Wolf as he continued to load bags of credits to the centre of the room, and in the entire time that was the extent of their conversation and at last they were ready.

****

Millie picked up Jack and the professor,

"How did it go?" she said, as they got in the craft,

"It all went to plan," smiled Jack, *"They jumped back 20 minutes ago, so on our timeline they will be ready to leave in an hour or so, are we ready this end?"*

"I think so," said Millie, *"We'll need to visit Danny soon, everyone is itching to get going,"*

"I think we'll lift everyone else to the safe house in the first run, the four of us plus maybe Danny on the second," said the professor,

"That's eight plus the pilot, we'll be heavy," said Jack,

"It's not a long haul flight," replied the professor, *"We'll manage, and anyway, the Danny scenario is between the four of us for now, best we keep it that way until we know."*

THAWOO and they were back in the east wing. Elspeth greeted them behind the mirror,

"Danny's on the prowl, best you all show your faces."

"Ok," said Jack, *"Danny will be reporting to control in 10 minutes, we'll accost him when he comes out of his quarters,"*

they waited until Danny went to report and Jack stood on a chair in the games room.

"Listen up people, we are ready to go, make your way to the sports hall, Millie will be there to help, you three stay here with me," he said pointing at the three other military guys in the east wing.

The rest filed out of the games room, and at the sports hall, Millie stood by the mirror.

"This way please, all aboard, just one in the cockpit seat, there are not enough seats, the two unlucky ones will strap themselves to the inside of the craft at the back using the belts provided."

Jack and his three cohorts waited for Danny to come out, and when he did, they overpowered him,

"What the hell?" he shouted as he was wrestled to the floor, *"Palmer, you'll pay for this,"*

His hands and then feet were bound and finally some tape placed over his mouth before they carried him to his bed and strapped him to it. The three men left Jack and ran onto the sports hall to join the others. Once everyone was in Millie took her seat, she checked and rechecked the dials, all was well.

"Ok, we are about to jump, we will start the engines, once we jump, there will be a drop and we are heavy, don't be alarmed," "Roger go on time," she mumbled to herself. *"Roger go on cords, ready to jump and jump,"* and with that, she hit the button.

THAWOO, immediately she started the engines, falling, she wrestled with the controls, still falling, until finally the ship began to level and then slowly climb, it was like driving a car with flat tyres, slow lumbering movements, the two extra people right at the back were making a difference, but she landed to applause from the passengers.

"We hope you enjoyed your flight, have a pleasant onward journey." Millie breathed a huge sigh of relief, halfway there she thought.

50
BOOMERANG

Wolf, Rocky, Zane and Jimmy had finished loading huge boxes full of credits to the middle of the room with an hour to spare, so they waited until their allotted time. THAWOO and they were back in the hideout, everything looked ok. Jimmy walked towards the door,

"Where do you think you're going?" said Wolf,

"I'm leaving," said Jimmy,

but Wolf bent down and pulled a revolver from under a drainage grill in the floor,

"Not another step," he shouted as he pointed the gun at Jimmy,

"We had a deal," said Jimmy,

"You got what you wanted, now I need to get going if I'm to have any chance of escape."

Wolf paused for a moment still pointing the gun,

"Ok," he said lowering his weapon,

"We had a deal,"

Jimmy breathed a sigh of relief, turned again and made for the door,

"Good luck Palmer,"

"You too Wolf."

Jimmy stepped outside and began to walk away.

"Pssss," came a voice from the shadows,

"Keep walking straight, to the gates, don't stop,"

Jimmy did as he was told, then from the shadows he was grabbed by the arm and pulled to the ground behind a car.

"I've got him," the man whispered over his shoulder.

The man was a swat team member, dressed completely in black, a sub machine gun hung from his shoulder,

"On your knees, you are going that way,"

he pointed, Jimmy did as he was told and crawled on his hands and knees in the direction indicated, he was soon lifted to his feet by two more of the swat team, escorted through some trees to a road where he saw an army of men taking cover behind cars and a bus shelter.

Back in the hideout, spirits were high,

"Look at all this Wolf, we're rich, woohoo," shouted Rocky,

"Nice one boss," said Zane,

"Ok, weapon up," said Wolf,

"We gotta load the van."

The two others took revolvers from the same drainage grill in the floor,

"Zane, see if the van is here, Rocky call Bull, find out where they are, get them back here,"

Wolf tossed Rocky the phone, and Zane went to the other end of the warehouse to another door to the outside. Zane saw the van in a corner of the car park in the rear of the warehouse, he opened the driver's side door and clambered in. He dropped the keys from the sun visor and 'click', the sound of a weapon cocking in his ear,

"Don't move," said the voice. Zane saw a man's head wearing a balaclava and a helmet, just behind his, in the rear view mirror.

"Hands up, slowly, now lock your fingers behind your head," Zane did as he was told, and he was soon in cuffs.

Another man then appeared, and they physically pulled Zane over the seats and into the back of the van, putting tape over his mouth, forcing him out the back doors and into the shadows.

"It's just ringing out boss," said Rocky,

"Try it again," said Wolf, and Rocky did, but again there was no reply.

"Something's up," said Wolf as he went to a window, looked left and right, all was quiet.

"Where is Zane?" he whispered before running to the other end of the warehouse and peering out; he could see the van but not Zane.

Something was definitely off he thought, and so he ran back picked up a rucksack, emptied what was left of its contents, grabbed a knife, jemmied open a crate, and began to fill the rucksack with credits. Rocky followed suit,

"What's up boss?"

"Something's off Rocky, go see if you can find Zane,"

Wolf sensed he was sending Rocky to certain capture or worse, but he needed to buy some time. Rocky ran to the other end of the warehouse pulling his rucksack over both shoulders, he took his revolver from the back of his pants and gingerly opened the door. Wolf filled a second rucksack, pulled the Bayze close to him, and at that moment, he heard the crack of gunfire outside. He looked at the machine for a moment then hit the jump button, THAWOOO and he was back in the safe in The Union Bank. He rolled the dials, but nothing happened. Unbeknown to him the boomerang switch had been activated, he hit the jump button again, THAWOOO and he was back in the hideout, but this time three armed figures were entering the front door, and over his shoulder four more coming in the back. Anywhere but here he thought! THAWOOO and he was back in the safe.

It was Saturday afternoon at 3:30pm, or so he thought, he would wait it out until the safe was opened at some point on Monday.

51
FLASH DRIVE

Millie arrived back in the east wing and went to find the others, they were sitting in the games room,

"All done," said Millie,

"Good work Millie," said Elspeth,

"Now let's go see Danny."

The two women found Danny where he had been left on the bed in his quarters, Elspeth sat in a chair at Danny's workstation, while Millie knelt by the side of the bed, and looked at him for a moment. He was sweating, his eyes red with tears, Millie was sad.

"Danny, I'm going to remove your gag, no screaming, there's no point, I want to talk to you, nod if you understand,"

Danny nodded as Millie pulled the tape carefully from Danny's mouth.

"What the hell Millie, you're not mixed up in this are you? And I'm very surprised at you Mrs Braithwaite," he said as he breathed heavily through his mouth.

"Now listen carefully Danny, we don't have much time,"

"No Millie," pleaded Danny, now in tears again.

"Listen," said Millie calmly, *"We are leaving, I like you, I always have, and I wanted to give you the chance to come with us, there's nothing left for you here,"*

"Oh Millie," said Danny, *"What have you got yourself mixed up in?"*

"Danny, do you want to come with me, that's the question?"

"Oh Millie," repeated Danny.

Millie looked over her shoulder, and Elspeth shook her head, Millie put the tape back over Danny's mouth,

"wait" said Danny in a muffled voice from behind his gag,

Millie removed the tape once more,

"It's called uncertainty", said Danny

"What?" said Millie puzzled

"Uncertainty, channel ZED Friday at nine"

Millie rolled her eyes and replaced the tape once more.

"I'll come back for you I promise," and with that the women left, and Danny rolled on his back, more tears.

"Not coming," said Millie as she marched past Jack and the professor, *"Let's get out of here."*

Elspeth followed behind, rolling her eyes, they all walked towards the craft, and the professor began to limp,

"You ok Freddie?" said Jack,

"Yeah," said the professor, *"An old injury, plays up when I'm stressed,"*

Jack took his place beside Millie in the cockpit,

"Cheer up Millie, it was for the best," he said.

Millie turned to him and forced a smile, Elspeth and the professor strapped in behind them.

"Oh no," said the professor, *"I've left a flash drive",*

"I'll get it," said Jack, *"You'll take forever with that leg,"* as he unbuckled and jumped to his feet, *"Where is it?"*

"In my cell on the bed." As soon as Jack left the craft, the professor jumped up and took Jack's place in the cockpit,

"What are you doing Freddie?" said Millie,

"Change of plan," said the professor, as he spun the dials, THAWOO and they were in The Palomino.

"No!" shouted Millie, as she wrestled the professor for control of the dials, THAWOOO, and they were back in

305

the east wing. Jack was rounding the corner of the mirror on his way back from retrieving the flash drive,

"Elspeth," shouted the professor,

Elspeth grabbed one of the belts that had been used earlier from the back of the craft, threw a loop over Millie's head down her body and pulled it tight, around her waist and arms just above her elbows, Elspeth secured it to the chair. Millie couldn't move her arms, she flailed her legs around, trying to kick the professor but couldn't reach the dials. Just as Jack was walking towards the craft, THAWOOO - they were gone. Jack stood looking bemused, there must have been a problem he thought, he would wait there for their return.

****

Palmer sat opposite Inspector Peterson in his office at the police station

"So Mr Palmer, can you tell us exactly what happened?",

"Well, I was doing my rounds, someone came up behind me, forced my arm up my back, and then pushed me into a room nearby, I think 1537,"

"Go on," said Peterson,

"There were three of them, they had some sort of machine on the table, I now know it to be a time machine, within minutes they were fiddling with the machine, and we were then in this huge room, we were tiny, there was a lot of waiting around, as we grew I could see it was a strong room of some kind although I don't know where,"

"That was the safe of the Union Bank," said Peterson helpfully, *"Continue…",*

"I know their names from their conversation, the leader was called Wolf, and the other two Zane and Rocky, they loaded a bunch of crates to an area in the safe, I'm pretty sure it was those escaped convicts who have been all over the telly, I helped them, I hope I'm not in trouble for that,"

"Don't worry about that Mr Palmer, please continue,"

"There's not much else to say, I lost track of time but eventually we arrived in a warehouse where you picked me up,"

"And how did you escape?" said Peterson,

"It was not so much an escape really, they were all in a good mood and quite distracted, I saw an opportunity to make for the door, but the leader pulled a gun on me. I told him I needed a pee, that bit was true, so he told me not to be long, and I walked out. Not sure if I'd try to run, I didn't even know where I was or when for that matter, they had guns, then your guy got me to safety."

Palmer was asked to describe the machine in as much detail as he could remember, Peterson took notes.

"And you'd never met these men before?"

"No, I knew of them, as I said, they've been all over the news, I also knew they were very dangerous, I feared for my life,"

"Yes, it's an awful experience, I think that will be all for now, do you have someone to look after you when you get home, where is home?"

"The Palomino, I live there, and you can get hold of me anytime you

wish, I'll leave my personal number, anything at all."

"Thank you very much for your help Mr Palmer, I'll get a squad car to drop you off."

In another room Zane sat opposite another officer,

"No comment," he said, and he would say that many times over in the coming hours.

Rocky was killed in the gun battle and Wolf was still sweating it out in the safe of The Union Bank. Peterson sat at his desk pondering the recent events when another officer walked in,

"He's not saying a word," he said referring to Zane,

"I'm not surprised," said Peterson,

"Get me an expert on time travel here as soon as possible,"

"Yes boss."

Peterson thought some more, Warden Phipps story stood up to scrutiny, after all they had caught or killed all but one of the escapees from Green River 8, his account had been accurate. Palmer also came up clean, no criminal record, his account was plausible, but how did they get their hands on a time machine, those things were like gold dust?

****

Jack waited for the return of his friends. In the Palomino sports hall Millie sat in the cockpit, still strapped in, still unable to move,

"Untie me and let me know what the hell is going on," she protested,

"First I need you to calm down," said the professor,

"I'll calm down when I'm good and ready," shouted Millie.

"LISTEN TO THE PROFESSOR," shouted Elspeth, so loud her voice reverberated around the inside of the craft.

Millie instantly fell silent, and the professor looked at Elspeth in shock,

"Now Freddie," said Elspeth calmly,

"Perhaps you'd like to explain to Millie what has just happened here."

The professor pulled a flash drive from his pocket, plugged it in, and the monitors flicked into life.

"Watch this," is all he said, and Millie saw footage of the first meeting between Jack and Jimmy,

"I've seen this, I was there remember?!" said Millie

The professor fast forwarded to the bit where Jack was showing off the craft.

"I remember," said Millie, *"Jack was like a secondhand car salesman,"*

"Listen to the audio, you'd been waiting remember, the lanthaneodinium had settled, its crystal clear."

He pressed play.

"The whole shell is one piece of carbon fibre and the wings are a plastic and silk mix, very strong, jeez Jimmy how long did it take you to build

that thing?"

The professor rewound the tape, and played it again,

"and silk mix, very strong, jeez Jimmy how long did it take you to build that thing?"

The professor rewound again as Millie watched on in horror,

"Jeez Jimmy how long did it take you to build that thing?"

"Jimmy is calling Jack Jimmy," she said finally.

"That's because Jack is not Jack at all,", said Elspeth.

"The Jack we know, our friend of over six years, the friend we trusted with our lives and our secrets, is Jimmy Palmer the serial killer."

Millie sat in silence for a moment, *"It can't be true,"* she said,

"I'm afraid it is," said the professor.

"Freddie showed me the recording," said Elspeth, *"I pulled some strings and got hold of his prison file, he's Jimmy alright, the guy you know as Jimmy is Jack although in the Palomino he goes by the name Jay as in J for Jack, I'm sorry Millie."*

Elspeth unbuckled Millie from the chair and leant over and cuddled her from behind, the professor lent over and touched Millie's knee,

"I'm truly sorry Millie," he said sincerely.

Millie held her head in her hands, numb with the pain of this new information, and she began to sob,

"How didn't I see this, how did I miss it?"

"Don't be hard on yourself honey, Freddie and I were equally shocked,"

"How long have you known?"

"Since this meeting, I watched the recording when you got back" said the professor, *"Although I knew something wasn't right when he kept watching the killings over and over."*

"So what will become of him?" said Millie,

"We thought that decision should be for the three of us," said the professor, *"He's in the right place now and he won't be getting out ever, if we hold his secret over him, he will keep quiet regarding Phipps, his brother, the extra time machine and everything else."*

"There's still one guy in jail for a crime Jimmy committed so we'll work on getting him out as a priority," said Elspeth,

"How many?" said Millie,

"Well," said the professor, *"There's the three we know about, we have probable cause for another seven and we are still digging."*

"Jeez, at least 10 then, he should get the chair,"

"I agree," said Elspeth, *"But let's not be hasty, we have a lot to lose if he spills the beans."*

****

Palmer sat and waited for over an hour for his friends to return, what had become of them he wondered? He pulled the flash drive from his pocket and looked at it, a quick look whilst I'm waiting, he thought. He headed down to Danny's quarters, the door still propped open with a bin, although he had the key card anyway. He stepped in and sat at Danny's workstation, Danny still laying on the bed across the room, watching. He pushed in the flash drive, the monitors flicked into life and on the screen in front of him sat the professor.

"Hello Jack, you are probably wondering what has become of us, all alone there with maybe just Danny for company. We won't be back for you I'm afraid and by now you should have figured out why."

Jack looked over at Danny, he paused the video, plugged in some earphones and pressed play again.

"Elspeth and I are very disappointed and by the time you are watching this Millie will also know and you know how she felt about Jimmy, don't you Jimmy? Anyway, we are going to keep your little secret for now as it would surely mean the chair for you if the authorities found out. We are not doing this for old times' sake, we are doing this for Phipps and his family, for your brother, and all the other inmates including us, on the east wing. If you keep our secret, we'll keep yours, you don't need to destroy the flash drive, this recording will play only once. I'd wish you luck, but I wouldn't mean it, goodbye".

The monitor went blank, Palmer pulled it from the drive and reinserted it, nothing, he tried everything, but the recording had disappeared, and the flash drive was empty. He pulled the keyboard from its housing and threw it against the wall, and it clattered to the floor, he put his head in his hands as Danny watched on, he was screwed.

52
RETIREMENT

"So, what do we do now?" said Millie,

"We are going to stay in The Presidential Suite here for a while until we see how everything plays out, the current guests are leaving today," said Elspeth.

"Jay has left some clothes for you somewhere, you two get changed, I need to pay Phipps a visit," and with that she was off.

At the suite she sat with Phipps and Nicki, Lucy ran in and out periodically,

"She's so sweet," said Elspeth, *"How did the news conference go today?"*

"It was great," said Phipps, *"They think I'm a hero, it's an exclusive, going out on the six o'clock news,"* he looked at his watch, not long now he thought.

"Ok, so you are all ready to leave, where would you like to go?"

"We'd like to go here," said Nicki pointing at the list.

"Ahh, a very good choice," said Elspeth smiling, *"That would have been mine,"* Nicki smiled too.

"Do you mind if I use your phone?" said Elspeth,

"Phone," said Phipps to the ceiling, *"Just tell it where you want to be connected,"*

"Oh," said Elspeth, clearing her throat. *"Goat Travel,"*

"Hey how can I help?",

"Number 7 please, first class, one way,"

"Very good thank you," click.

"What about our new identities?" said Nicki,

"You will travel to the airport and pick up tickets at the desk in your name to Ontario, clear customs with your passports. Airside, you alone Mr Phipps, will go to the Kangaroo bar, order something to drink and wait, you will be approached by a man who is not dissimilar to you in frame and build. He will ask you if you have ever been to Australia, and this is your cue to leave your passports and tickets with him. He in turn will leave your new identities and tickets with you."

"That's amazing," said Nicki, and Elspeth smiled,

"It's time for you to go, you'll be another 12 hours growing back to full size, so we thought a trip in the middle of the night would be a little easier, everyone's a bit less on the ball. Are you ready?"

"I can't say I won't miss this place," said Phipps, and they all took in their surroundings,

"It's quite nice I suppose," said Elspeth, I can't wait to move in, she thought.

She joined the others,

"Fancy a drink at the big bar, we've got to wait for the room?"

"I fancy some non-prison food," said Millie,

"Jay will join us later, but not out here, he'll join us in the room."

Millie looked a little puzzled, she was still getting used to her new reality without Jack, well with a new Jack to be precise and the new Jack was every bit the man the old Jack had been, without the habit of killing people whenever the urge arose. Millie would learn this once they got to know each other better.

Inspector Peterson sat with the time travel expert - a Professor Archibald Slim,

"We first need to establish what machine they have been using, it is very likely the TTm1, they come up on the black market and are most commonly used,"

Peterson reached for his notes. *"We have a description,"* he said, *"Silver in colour, two dials, about the size of two standard house bricks, does that help, there's more?"*

"Wow," said the expert, *"It's a Bayze, there are only seven known to be in existence, that's remarkable,"*

"And who owns them?"

"Governments, as far as anybody knows, does this guy know how to use it?"

The phone rang, *"Peterson, when? Ok keep me posted."* Peterson put the phone down,

"He's just turned up at the hideout, for a brief second, right next to one of my officers, he looked around, hit a button and disappeared again,"

"You mean he jumped back to exactly the same spot as he had jumped to before?"

"Well the same building, I'm not sure if it was exactly the same spot."

"Hmmm…" said the expert, *"He has the perfect tool for escape, he can go anywhere he wants, at any time, if he knows what he's doing, it sounds to me as if the boomerang switch is activated,"*

"Boomerang switch?" enquired Peterson,

"It was a safety feature on the Bayze. It's a switch on the side of the machine, barely imperceivable in the casing unless you know what you are looking for. The switch fixes the location and time you are going from and the location and time you are going to, so each time you hit the switch you travel between the two. The dials won't work unless the switch is deactivated, tell me what you know about the other location?",

"Well that's the safe of The Union Bank,"

"And the when?", "About one in the morning so, 16 hours ago and counting,"

"Ok, so provided he doesn't figure it out, in which case you'll never catch him, well not until a time tremor shows up, that's where he is

now, or rather that's where he was, and he will be in one of only those two locations."

****

Wolf threw the machine down in front of him, he needed to think, he still hadn't figured out that every time he jumped when he came back, he effectively started again timewise. Wolf travelled back to the hideout several more times to the same spot. Peterson instructed the officers to move out of sight and wait. On his last trip back, Wolf looked around, nobody there, it was a chance at freedom here or the prison that was the safe. He stood up slowly, nobody, he moved towards the window, nothing outside, he would leave out the back, he thought, he crept quietly until he reached the door, he opened it slowly and was outside. The fresh air filled his lungs, but no sooner had he taken a breath, he was met with blinding lights, "Drop the case," a number of red dots appeared on his chest, "Drop the case" the voice repeated. Wolf put the case down and raised his hands, and men came from every angle and bundled him to the floor, the game was up.

****

"Your room is ready now" said the woman standing at Elspeth's table,

"Great," she said, *"I need a bath, come on you two, let's get comfortable,"* it was now 5:30pm.

****

Jimmy decided it was time to untie Danny, and as soon as

he did, Danny raised the alarm. Almost immediately, the east wing filled with guards, and Jimmy was thrown to the floor and then to the cooler,

"They've all gone except him," said Danny.

Sirens and red lights flashed everywhere, and Danny was taken to the infirmary to be checked over. He was later to be admonished for the whole debacle, but he escaped any formal charge, all focus was on why a decision had been taken at a senior level to have only one guard looking after an entire wing, regardless of the number of inmates. Danny's career in the prison system was over.

****

Peterson was sitting at his desk when Wolf's arresting officer walked in,

"Good job",

"Thank you sir,"

"Now where's this machine everybody has been making all the fuss about?"

"FBI took it sir, I got a receipt," he said fumbling in his pocket.

"Receipt?" said Peterson, *"What the hell are the FBI doing getting involved in this?",*

"You can ask yourself sir, one of them is here to see you," and with that a man wearing dark glasses appeared at the office door and flashed his credentials.

"Come in, take a seat, Agent?"

"Cragg,"

"Take a seat Agent Cragg." The agent sat down,

"Inspector Peterson, you and your men are to be congratulated for the apprehension of this gang, you've done a fine job, but we are going to take it from here."

"What?" said Peterson,

"I'm afraid so, you won't see it on the news but there's been another breakout, 11 inmates, all time travel offenders. The important thing is we have got the machine,"

"Well you won't get anything out of the two we've got sitting in the cells, they're saying nothing."

"I know, the one traveller left behind is equally tight lipped, but we have a very sophisticated piece of technology that processes billions of data sets every second looking for time tremors, that's our best chance of tracking these people down now, you don't have the skills or resources here to do the job,"

"Now wait a minute," said Peterson,

"Inspector," said the agent, *"These travellers were experienced, they probably jumped back a week maybe even a month ago, which means they could quite literally be anywhere in the world right now, and if they are careful in that first period of time, chances of catching them are slim to say the least."*

"And this time tremor software of yours, anything there?"

"A small tremor down in Venezuela, we are checking it out now, as I say, the important thing is we have the machine, it's a top of the range

319

piece of kit, we have been involved at a presidential level in speaking to each of the governments who own one of these things. Understandably nobody is admitting that they lost theirs, but we've got it now, and the big wigs are mighty pleased about that, you're up for a medal Inspector, a fine job, well done."

****

Elspeth, Millie and the professor, all scrubbed up very well and were sitting in one of the vast living spaces, one sofa each, waiting for Phipps broadcast on the six o'clock news. A news flash showing Backman's capture was broadcast just before 6:00pm to the woops and cheers of the three travellers, then Phipps.

"We now have an exclusive interview with the hero of the hour, Warden Joshua Phipps who was instrumental in bringing these five criminals back to justice," more cheers.

Phipps went on to explain his emergency operation, his convalescence, and the chance meeting in the big bar whereby he discovered the gang's plan. When asked about the kidnapping he said,

"It's just awful, I'm pleased he's home safe," and the deaths of three of the gang, *"Well of course it's sad when anyone loses their life but the brave men and women of the NYPD put themselves in the firing line every day, and I understand at least one of our fine officers was wounded in the exchange, these men were extremely dangerous individuals,"* and what next *"I'm going to retire, at times like this you realise how important family is, the gang could have spotted me at any moment as I waited to get the full details of their dreadful plan, so I'm going to spend more time with my family."*

The travellers applauded at the end of the broadcast,

"He was good," said Elspeth,

"Very good," agreed the others,

"Excuse me madam, you have a visitor,"

"Ah, that's Jay," said Elspeth, *"Bring him in,"* and before too long Jay was in the room, the three travellers stood to greet him.

"Elspeth, Freddie, and you must be Millie, I've heard so much about you and I am honoured to finally meet you, I'm Jack Palmer but people around here call me Jay,"

Millie got up, held out her hand and did a slight curtsy, Elspeth looked at the floor and smiled.

"I'm pleased to meet you too Jay, did you know for a long time we thought you were your brother?"

"I did, and I'm sure you weren't too keen, what with everything we now know,"

"You can say that again." said Millie,

"but my friends tell me you've got all the good bits Jack had, I mean Jimmy had, I'll get used to it" they all smiled.

"We've not really had a chance to talk about that Jay, how are you feeling?" said Elspeth,

"Well Jimmy was always a concern for the family, I knew my dad hadn't done the deed, I always knew in my heart of hearts but, we were both shipped off to care so quickly, and in those early days all we had

321

was each other,"

"Well, you've got us now," said the professor, *"I thought we would eat outside, the weather is lovely,"* he winked at Jay, and Jay smiled as they made their way to the outdoor sundecks.

A table was laid for four and glasses of champagne had been freshly poured, Elspeth picked up a glass,

"To us," she said,

"To us." they said in unison.

"Hey Jay?" said Elspeth, *"We're hiring, Freddie here wants to build another machine, some updates apparently and so were going to need another pilot, you can keep your job here too, interested?"*

Jay smiled, *"Well hell yeah."*

Freddie looked at the ceiling,

"Warm dark night, fireworks," and with that the skies darkened, at least for those in the presidential suit, fireworks began to go off, claps and sparkles of every colour imaginable until you could barely see sky for the display,

"To wherever, whenever," said the professor,

"Wherever, whenever," said the other three as they clinked their glasses and watched the night sky.

****

A man sat stationary in the driver's seat of his yellow taxicab in the pouring rain, looking at the picture of Phipps beaming back at him from his news tablet. He was good with faces, he really thought he recognised the guy, probably a fare at some point. He was deep in thought when a woman knocked on the driver's side window,

"Can you take me to Connecticut?"

"Sure hop in," Connecticut he thought, this was sure to be a good ride a few hundred bucks at least, he'd never been to Connecticut, or had he?

- The End -

Printed in Great Britain
by Amazon